ROMAN WEDDING

ROMAN'S ADVENTURES, BOOK 4

By

Amber Anthony

Copyright

Paperback 978-1-73-438224-2
eBook 979-8-20-111629-3
Library of Congress Control Number: 2022909896

Credits
Edited by Michelle's Edits
Cover Artist: Kelly Ann Martin, kam.design
Roman Samborskyi (Dreamstime.com), foto76 (DepositPhotos),
silvae (DepositPhotos), -Robbie- (DepositPhotos), Gera8th (DepositPhotos),
Svetography (Shutterstock)

Published by Amber Anthony, Pickerington Ohio
Printed in the United States of America

The Roman Family Mai Tai

Served at Twin's Tavern, Pickerington Ohio
Thank you, David Brucas,
for your heavenly bartending hand.

1 1/2 ounces white rum

3/4-ounce orange curaçao

3/4-ounce lime juice, freshly squeezed

1/2 ounce orgeat*

1/2-ounce dark rum

Garnish: lime wheel

Garnish: mint sprig

- Add the white rum, curaçao, lime juice, and orgeat into a shaker with crushed ice and shake lightly (about 3 seconds).
- Pour into a double rocks glass.
- Float the dark rum over the top.
- Garnish with a lime wheel and mint sprig.

*Orgeat syrup is a sweet syrup made from almonds, sugar, and rose water or orange flower water. It was originally made with a barley-almond blend. It has a pronounced almond taste and is used to flavor many cocktails. *Orgeat syrup is a vital ingredient in the Mai Tai.*

Dedication

We dedicate this book to our loyal family of readers and peers who inspire us.

To those who experienced disappointment or loss in a first love but live in the hope of finding love again.

Thank you, Michelle, for your third set of eyes.

CHAPTER ONE

The Hawaiian Air Flight attendant approached the woman in row thirty-six, seat B. "Excuse me, ma'am, may I see your boarding pass?"

The executive, already wearing her 'Girl Boss' sleep mask, lifted the leopard print shade carefully. "I beg your pardon?"

Ava Hansen, the rightful owner of seat thirty-six B, looked everywhere but at the skirmish that was about to unfold. With a great deal of harrumphing, the thirty-something girl boss unbuckled and made a big deal out of pulling her purse from the overhead bin.

With a kind, "Thank you, Luana," Ava nodded to the flight attendant. She settled herself in the seat she'd come to think of as her own during the three months of wrangling it took to sell her Las Vegas home. She slid her precious Louboutin shopping bag under the seat in front of her and prepared for utter relaxation.

As she opened her ereader, she spied the man across the aisle in thirty-five C stretching out wonderfully long legs. He let out a sigh and folded his arms over his chest. His biceps tried the fabric of his white polo shirt. *Man, he has a tan.* She wanted to check his left hand for a ring, but she was on the wrong side of the plane.

What am I doing? And why isn't the seat next to him my favorite? This is the first time I've checked out a man in a decade. I take this flight all the time. I've never seen him before. … Steel-grey hair like James Brolin… clipped military conservative. Nice shoes. You can tell a lot about a guy by their shoes.

Ava chomped at the bit to retrieve her nice shoes from the bag in front of her feet. As soon as the alert permitted, she pulled the double Louboutin shopping bag to her lap and opened the box of the most expensive shoes she'd ever bought. *Well, one pair was.*

Ava smiled, almost in tears, holding a real-life glass slipper. She balanced the flat ballerina pump on the palm of her hand. The pointed toe slip-on was adorned with hand-placed shimmering crystals from toe to heel. The vamp, crafted from mesh, gave a nude look as if her foot was bejeweled. Turning it to confirm the shoe was really hers, she caressed the ultra-luxurious feel of the suede wrapped heel. The woman next to her gasped and Ava asked her seatmate, "Have you ever seen such a beautiful shoe in your life?"

The traditional Hawaiian auntie grinned. "I'd have nowhere to wear them."

Ava held the shimmering flat to her heart. "I splurged on them for work because a client told me how comfortable these are." Ava felt that handsome man's gaze and turned to see the warmest pair of brown eyes smiling back at her. The gold in his eyes raised their heat to elemental magic. With a nod to him, she carefully placed the ecru silk shoe back in its box. She turned back to Auntie. "…And I was terrible because I bought their crystal-covered big sister." Ava opened the second box and dangled the delicate slingback pump on her index finger. "I feel so indulgent."

In the airplane's downlight, the pump's pale silk mesh upper sparkled with a gradient design of hand fixed Swarovski iridescent crystals. The seventy-millimeter heel was not this brand's highest nor lowest slim heel. The red sole kissed it with an enchanted touch.

The Hawaiian woman grinned. "A'a i ka hula, waiho i ka maka'u i ka hale."

Ava narrowed her gaze. "That's something about dancing, right?"

With cheerful eyes, the woman's lyrical voice translated, "Dare to dance, leave shame at home."

Ava sighed. "You don't know how much I needed to hear that." She put the shoes away and thought about the proverb. *I can hear the backstabbers now. 'She spent all that money after selling the house Sheldon built for her.'* Ava contemplated the seven-figure sale. *If they knew Sheldon, they'd understand he finagled three mortgages on it. The Louboutins and the cost of the trip was the entirety of my net profit.* "Thank you for being so gracious." She felt her voice catch, working hard not to let her emotions spill over. As she sat up from stowing her treasures, she caught Mr. Handsome sneaking another peek at her. This time, she smiled, and he winked.

Ava was at once gratified and alarmed. She needed to dial it back. She did not wish to be conspicuous. For all she knew that big, strapping tower of lean muscle was a Fed tailing her back to Hawaii.

****

Ava considered the personalities of the people at the baggage carousel. Half of them impatiently clogged the standing room where the bags belched out. The other half meandered to the far side where they waited and watched the scrappier flyers scrambling for their bags.

There was Mr. handsome on the other side of the carousel, every bit of the six-foot-three she imagined him to be. *He has to be a Fed. He's keeping me in his line of sight while appearing blasé.*

Ava readjusted her tote-sized purse on her shoulder and dropped the Louboutin shopping bag at her feet. She had tagged her bright-pink luggage as 'fragile' and expected the two pieces painted with hummingbirds and poppies to arrive early.

Leaning over to catch the first bag, Ava heard the crowd rumbling behind her. A hubbub arose with the scuffles. 'Stop him!' She gaped in confusion as she was pushed onto the carousel. Then fury blossomed as some asshole ran off with her Louboutin bag.

Time froze. Though she scrambled to right herself, she rode the carousel, gripping her smaller suitcase and screaming, "Stop this thing!" *And now they're all looking at me. This belt moves faster than it looks.*

People yelped and drew back as Mr. Handsome took two steps to his right, stuck out a strong arm, and clothes-lined the asshole with her bag. She watched it all in slow motion. He was gracefully powerful, and said not so much as a word.

The crowd clapped as the man grabbed the criminal's neck and pushed him face-first onto the cold floor. Two airport security officers arrived in seconds; just in time for Mr. handsome to hand off the criminal and hand her the shopping bag. The belt screeched to a stop. Those brown eyes of his smiled as he held out his hand. "May I help you off that thing?"

All obscurity lost, she accepted his hand and gathered her dignity. "Yes, thanks." The crowd still gawked as Ava raised her chin and announced to the gathering throng. "Nothing to see here. Go about your business." She nodded to the hostesses, greeting people with flowered necklaces. "Go get leid."

When she'd donned her beige linen trousers and tunic last night for the red-eye flight, it was the plainest clothing she owned, perfect for disappearing in a crowd. She looked around and grinned painfully as she accepted her shopping bag. "Are you a cop? Amazing reflexes there."

"No, ma'am, just a man happy to help a lady in distress."

She let go of his hand, realizing she'd held it too long.

"I'm Hank…"

Yeah, sure you are. She nodded and answered. "I'm… Ava."

He looked for security in the crowd. "I don't know if you had plans after landing, but I'm sure security will want a statement from both of us."

They watched the process of authorities surrounding the thief and Ava clutched the shopping bag. "Oh, cheese and crackers, they'll want my shoes as evidence."

The stranger took a commanding stance to half-block her from view. He spoke back at her over his shoulder. "They might. Can you stow those shoes in your tote bag?"

Leaving the boxes and the receipt for twenty-four hundred dollars' worth of shoes in the bag, Ava waited silently with Mr. handsome.

****

Ava and the stranger left the security office together. She dug for her keys. "I have my car; may I drop you somewhere?"

He smiled, and it went all the way to those coffee-brown eyes. "No, ma'am, I've got a rental waiting for me." He looked at his watch. "It's about time for brunch. Would you meet me somewhere?"

The hair on the back of Ava's neck rose in alarm. How had she forgotten this man could be surveilling her? How else could he have been so reactive to her assault? "Aren't you sweet to offer?" She began evasive maneuvers away from him. "I'm afraid my schedule won't allow for brunch." Now she was arm's length away. "Thank you so much for the rescue today." She pressed the elevator button for the parking level. "Have a wonderful time in Hawaii." She bolted as the elevator doors opened.

****

In the safety of her locked car, Ava settled down to the task of navigating the tourist traffic to Waikiki. What *if* the Feds were following her? She was headed home, and they knew where that was. They'd made her life an obstacle course for almost five years. Since the statute of limitations on the millions Sheldon had stolen was evaporating, they'd become dogged in their surveillance.

Hell, did the Feds buy my Las Vegas home to tear it apart looking for the money? A van cut her off, and she snapped her attention back to driving. She saw the bumper sticker for Aloha Travel and wondered, *where did Sheldon Carmichael go with his ill-gotten gains?*

She'd torn the house apart without success. She'd had no choice but to wait the regulation five years to have him declared legally dead. *The joke is on the Feds if consider me their chief suspect in his disappearance.*

****

US Major General Henry 'Hank' Kingston settled into his rental car and cranked up the A/C. It took stopping at the first traffic signal out of the airport before the reality of his retirement sunk in. He was a free man on the island of Oahu. Four extra years in Afghanistan put a second star on his shoulder and more wiggle room in his retirement pay. More money to explore bachelorhood and the exciting ratio of ninety-four men for every one hundred women in his age range.

It wasn't that widower Hank had been a monk for those long years, but at his rank, it wouldn't do to fraternize. There hadn't been a significant woman in his life for the last six years. *Boy, did I bomb out with that beautiful blonde! I saved her damn shoes and couldn't score a brunch date. Ah well, I'll sit by the pool at the condo and meet my neighbors. Besides, I want Sky to know I'm settling in.*

Sky Kingston, his daughter, and only child, met her match on the island in a confluence of circumstances. What were the odds that she would sit next to his best friend's son on the flight over? They fell in love at first sight and now Hank was preparing to pay for a wedding. Sky and Conner were making their home in Waikiki. Hank gave them a little grace by living in a different neighborhood, a few floors below his best friend in Mo'ili'ili. So what if it was a neighborhood adjacent to Waikiki?

He stepped inside his twenty-fifth-floor three-bedroom condo. He hadn't had this much space since he was a Captain at Minot A.F.B. That was ages ago when Dory was pregnant with Sky. *Then I had to share the space with a nursery and Dory's book club. Today, it's all mine. What if I don't install a home phone? What if I forget to publish my cell number? What if I just enjoy the peace and quiet and women?*

Despite his best intentions, sleep eluded the keyed-up sixty-six-year-old who looked nowhere near his age. Nevertheless all his military physical fitness did not protect him from the effects of too much scotch at his retirement send-off last night.

His cool shower washed the travel grime away with the scent of *what did the bottle say? Swagger?* He ran his hands through his still full head of steel-grey hair, and it stood up spiky with swagger. *I like it.*

He ran a hand over his jaw and contemplated a beard. He'd never had facial hair. *Maybe I'll just go wild. It will probably itch, but what the, hey. I'm retired.* He kept the razor in the medicine cabinet, just in case.

Puttering around the condo, he observed the newly delivered living and dining room furniture. Between Sky and Conner, they had arranged things to maximize his 'travel brochure' views of the Waikiki skyline. The ivory walls awaited a collection of art and commemorative photos. They still leaned against the unpacked boxes in the third bedroom. Hank settled on the lanai's chaise for two. *It's too lonely.* Leaning over the railing, he was disappointed. No one was at the pool. *I'm bored.* He looked at his watch and realized it was nearly lunchtime.

****

A walk over the McCully Street bridge put him in the heart of Waikiki. *Maybe a full stomach and hair of the dog will put me down for a nap.* The tavern beckoned him with the sign, "Ugliest bartenders in town, best garlic shrimp ever."

Inside, the highlights of mainland baseball games played on big screen televisions, providing the majority of light. Coming in from the bright Honolulu sunshine, he felt like a mole stumbling in the near darkness. He caught the silhouette of the bartender and moved toward the empty barstool.

As he looked around at the clientele, he saw businesspeople at lunch in the booths. Hank sat and waited for his eyes to adjust to the dim hanging lights cut from empty tequila bottles. The one other occupant at the bar was a woman wearing a wide-brimmed hat. The globe light over her emphasized the white straw and the dark shadow surrounding her. The soft fabric of her native-print tunic split below her hip to reveal tapered slacks and strappy-heeled sandals. By the decorated straw purse at her feet, Hank guessed they were of the same generation.

She's on vacation, too. What the heck, this has worked before. He nodded to the bartender. "I'd like a Bulleit Bourbon and send one of whatever the lady is drinking down with my compliments."

"Sir, before you go through the motions. I have one question for you." The man wrung the bar mop in his hands as he gave Hank a questioning brow.

Hank sat back; hands folded. "You want to see my ID?"

The bartender shook his head with a smirk. "No. What's your preference in baseball? National or American League? That drink you're sending hangs on your answer."

Hank raised a brow. "What if I am not a fan at all?"

There was a general groan from the regulars behind him. The bartender leaned across the bar. "Care to reconsider?"

Hank looked at the Greek chorus around him. He felt their scrutiny as if they were sending psychic vibrations. He sensed he was the latest on the quest and the bartender was the troll guarding the bridge.

After the morning I've had? Oh, hell, go for broke. Hank smacked his palm on the bar and announced. "National League, because the American League are the pussys with designated hitters."

One of the chorus barked in anguish. Hank spun to his accuser, hands up in resignation. "Hey, buddy, it is what it is."

The woman picked herself up and moved two more barstools away from Hank. "Morty, change that channel to the Pirates and the Cubs."

There was a general groan from the National League supporters when the bartender did what she asked.

****

Ava Hansen recognized Mr. Handsome. Hank, she recalled. *Second strike, Hank. First, I think you're a Fed. Now I know you aren't a baseball lover.* That was just sad. But then, she had no particular love for football, and many considered that treasonous. She was amused by his bravado. She admired his broad chest. His Aloha shirt fit nicely and could not have hidden a badge or gun. *Is he IRS? Am I just being paranoid?*

She pondered this man from her cone of darkness. *Still virile in his sixties, check. His face is ruggedly handsome and tanned, check.* The smile lines around his eyes bore pale creases where he'd spent years squinting into the sun.

Ava crooked her finger at Morty. "Reward the gentleman with a consolation prize. Send over another of whatever he's drinking and make it a double."

The man's steely-brown gaze picked up from his one drink and he cocked his head, listening. His hand passed a gentle denial. "One's my limit at lunch, Ava. Even off duty." He looked directly into Ava's bright eyes. "How's your schedule? Got time for pork and ginger meatballs?"

Ava's mouth dropped open. He had her dead to rights. Still, she was fairly certain he hadn't followed her here. Is this a case of, *'of all the gin joints, in all the towns, in all the world, he walks into mine?'*

She glanced at her watch and smiled. "How did you find me?"

Hank's grin spread. "Find you? I just found the first bar closest to my place. Now, about those meatballs…"

Ava spun her barstool around. *Fight versus flight kicked in. Or is it indecision?* "I would love to, but unfortunately, I have an appointment in ten minutes." She grabbed up folders and slid them into a portfolio.

"What about some other day? You name it, I'll be here."

"Okay, Mr. Reliable. See you the day after tomorrow." She waggled her fingers over her shoulder as she threw open the door and blinded everyone with the outside light.

****

After her brief appointment, Ava returned to her condo. *What a day! What part of her heart or her brain sparked her to notice Hank?* In her quiet bedroom, she fell against the back of her vanity chair as she sliced open another envelope from her Las Vegas attorney. These constant legal inquiries aged her soul. She studied the worry lines between her brows as she dialed her attorney's office.

Victor Barry, commonly known as 'Victor Victorious' among the Vegas legal elite, got right to the point without pleasantries. "Good news. I got a letter today. You have been officially cleared of any suspicion in the matter of Sheldon Carmichael's disappearance and his financial crimes."

"Oh! Does that mean they've declared him dead?"

Victor's sigh was audible over several thousand miles. "No, dear, that's an entirely different matter."

Ava nearly snorted. "He's rooming with Jimmy Hoffa. Did it take Hoffa's widow this long?" She heard Victor's chair squeak as he sat back at his desk.

"It takes every spouse this long. It's the law."

"Then it's a good thing I had an in with that TV producer. Getting started in my business five years ago saved me. No one in Hawaii knew Sheldon Carmichael was my husband."

Victor's voice went silken. "Oh, part of the purpose of this call is to say I truly enjoyed our dinner at Delmonico's."

"Yes, that was a surprise." Ava blinked at the change of subject and how pleasant Victor's invitation to dinner was. They had spent two hours without talking business, just reminiscing about the 'over-the-top' past parties. By dessert, they'd counted themselves grateful to be the 'survivors'.

"You had to celebrate the sale of a home."

"Victor, that was no home. Home is where you want to be and, frankly, I'm home now."

"Hawaii agrees with you. I've never seen you so radiant."

"You ain't seen nothing yet. Once Sheldon is declared dead, I've got no strings."

"Surely, you don't think of every string related to Sheldon as a shackle?"

Ava sniffed. "Name one that isn't."

"What about me? Am I a shackle?"

Guilt rolled over her for not recognizing Victor's long conversation for what it was. *His wife is dead. My spouse is somewhere out there if he wasn't fed to the sharks.* "I believe the islands are the perfect place to find yourself. That's what I'm doing. Concentrating on me and my business." Ava closed her eyes. *He's courting me. Oh, hell, no.*

"From the buzz, you're the real deal in Oahu event planning."

"I can't believe my success has come in only five years. When they offered me a contract to cater a show in Hawaii it was a dream come true. I wasn't getting any younger, and Vegas is hell for anyone over nineteen." Ava smiled into the mirror.

Victor's smile came through his voice on the phone. "Well, kid, ya done good. This is where I say aloha?"

"That's right, aloha. Thanks for the good news. It takes a lot of pressure off me."

She closed the call and thought *I'll be more jovial when I meet with the general's daughter about her wedding tomorrow. Over the phone, the man is friendly. I'm going to give him the best event for his daughter, on a retiree's budget.*

Chapter Two

After Skylar Kingston dried her hands, she waved a dishtowel at her fiancé. "When Dad gets in this morning, he's picking up his rental car and we'll bring dinner over after he's had time to rest."

Conner Roman Jameson, the cowboy who'd won her heart before they both started college in Honolulu, stood up and carried his mug to the sink. Conner was the last of the Roman family men to set hearts aflutter at his family's fitness center. Work at the fitness center was something he'd leave behind as soon as the ink dried on the credentialing that made him a pilot and forty-nine percent owner of Kingston Air.

By the end of September, Sky and Conner would be married and working. Now, amid the excitement of graduation, they were headed to Sky's art studio to meet her mentor.

Sky shouldered her purse and asked Conner, "Would you drive? I'm keyed-up this morning."

Conner grabbed her and puckered up for a kiss. "Yeah, it's been a while since your dad has seen his baby girl."

As they made their way to his truck, Sky sighed. "I always feel like I'm twelve when I see him."

Conner smirked. "I'm here to tell you, you're all grown up." He wagged his eyebrows at her.

Sky raised her brow. "I guess I am…"

****

Sky folded her arms over her painting smock and cast an exasperated gaze at her mentor, Rando Kane. She gestured to her life-sized portrait of Hawaii's Queen Liliuokalani. "It's not right. It's still not right. It's flat." She threw her palms up to her forehead and ground out a groan of frustration.

Conner stood back, scratching his neck. He recognized that sound. It was the one she made when he thought everything looked great, and she still wasn't happy. He searched for words to soothe her frustration, but with Rando there, he wasn't able to offer the usual oral consolation. "Well, it's… I mean…"

Rando tipped his head to Conner and gave a small shake before he put an arm around Sky's shoulders and whispered. "You know what this is? It's been coming since you picked up your first paintbrush."

Sky's expression darkened. "What? Am I done as an artist? Do I get so many brush strokes before I wash out?" The almost twenty-four-year-old prodigy let out a heavy sigh and worked her way out of Rando's embrace. She threaded her fingers into her loose cream-soda-blonde hair and grunted. "You can tell me. I'm about to graduate with a business degree. I have other options."

Conner rolled his eyes and spun on one foot to face the back of the studio. He regarded her paintings selling for six figures, lined up like paratroopers ready to fly out the door. Among them were many commissioned portraits of rock stars, politicians, and children of the world's wealthiest families. "Darlin' you haven't hit the wall yet."

Rando winced and issued a time-out signal. "Sky, you want this portrait to exemplify the tone of the European portrait masters. You've certainly studied their style, but there's a difference between seeing it in a book and studying those brush strokes up close. You never had the opportunity to study glazes beside Leonardo DaVinci."

Sky's fists fell to her slim hips, and she whipped away from the two men who adored her. "So, now I need time travel?"

Conner looked skyward, his thumbs hooked in his belt loops as he paced behind his emotional love. "Oh, stop it." He caught her shoulders, gently cupping them from behind as he turned her back to Rando.

Rando gave her his best mentor stare. "My friend, Dmitriy Volkov, teaches DaVinci's sfumato technique in Florence. After your wedding, he has a ten-day intensive class. If you feel your portrait is missing depth, his class should punch up your expertise."

Conner made direct eye contact with Rando and gestured 'cut.' "I didn't want to spoil my surprise." He caught Sky's hands in his and his cowboy grin emerged. "I was saving this secret for last, but our honeymoon is in Rome. We could take the train to Florence, I could relax while you paint your little fingers off, then we have a transatlantic cruise back to Fort Lauderdale."

Sky bounced on the balls of her feet. "This is what you and Aunt Jordan were whispering about all these months?"

Conner nodded. "Yeah, then we fly home."

****

The next day, Hank pulled his rental into traffic and looked at Sky and Conner in the back seat. "Don't get used to being chauffeured. They're delivering my new car this week, and it's a two-seater. By the way, where is this hotel that's going to demand a formidable amount of my retirement money?"

"Oh, Daddy, you said you wanted the best." Sky scolded. Conner tucked his chin and swiveled to look at the passing traffic.

"We're headed to the Royal what?"

"The Royal Ohana. Just a few blocks up. Look for the statues of the Hawaiian Royal family out front." Sky leaned between the front seats and pointed.

Hank checked the time. "We are eating our way through this day."

"The planner ordered a selection of small plates to discuss the menu." Sky settled back into Conner's embrace. "It's not a six-course prime rib dinner."

Hank slowed as they approached the valet entry. "Conner, how many prospective clients do we expect from Kingston Air at this shindig?"

Conner winced. "I sat down with Kirk, and he redlined about half of my list. I expect seventy-five to one hundred."

He glanced in the rear-view mirror at his daughter. "And how many patrons are from your gallery?"

Sky answered brightly. "About the same."

Hank nodded. "So, including Air Force brass and guests, another seventy-five to one hundred. I say we give them a pack of peanuts, a half a can of soda, and thank them for coming."

Conner spoke up. "Sir? We have a better menu planned on our charter flights."

Hank rolled to a stop and turned to exit the car. "Right, and charter customers pay. Let's have the reception in the hangar."

"Dad, again, we don't have to do this at all." Sky got a little pouty as the valet opened her door.

They stood under the porte-cochere and took in the rarified air of the luxurious Waikiki beachfront resort. Hank threw an arm around Sky and squeezed her for emphasis. "Oh, Peanut, I'm just kidding. This is a big shindig, for business and pleasure."

The resort staff nodded and greeted them, directing them to a corner table in the dining room. Hank stopped in his tracks when he saw the woman at the round table. Hank's grin grew across his tanned face.

She looked up from her menus, and gasped. "Oh, my gosh, it's you!"

Sky turned to look at her father, bright eyes wide. "You two have met?"

Hank grinned. "In a manner of speaking. Are your shoes safe?" Ava's sparkling smile returned as she nodded. He met her nod with a conspiratorial smile. "I'll bet this time you let me pay for everything."

Ava stood professionally and extended her hand. "Ava Hansen, owner, and chief planner with Hau'oli-She Lives Aloha Events. You must be General Kingston, the father of the bride."

"Like I said at the bar, Ava, call me Hank. What do you have in store for us? I see lots of space on this table."

He sat at the table for eight as Ava exchanged pleasantries with Sky and Conner. She turned back to Hank. "Oh, plenty of food is coming. Sky and Conner filled out the entire questionnaire."

****

As small plates arrived, Ava began their grazing with questions. "We haven't discussed seating at the ceremony and reception. Are you keeping the traditional bride and groom seating at the ceremony?"

Conner and Sky looked at each other, nodding. Hank put down his fork. "We have a cobbled-together family on both sides. For Sky, there's me, and her aunt and uncle who raised her in Florida." He took a sip of sparkling water as Ava wrote. "Our side will be filled with art gallery patrons." His gaze moved to Conner. "The guy with the big appetite has his dad and step-mom, his brother, Jax, and Jax's wife, Kameo, and his mom and her husband, coming from Daytona Beach."

Ava nodded. "You mentioned a group from…" She checked her notes. "Kingston Air?"

Conner wiped his lips. "Kingston Air will make its debut flight on August first. They'll be on the groom's side."

Ava made notes and scrolled back on her tablet. "And your father is Kirk Roman with Silver Seal Fitness?" Her smile widened at the statement.

"That's my dad." Conner laughed. "Are you telling me you've never heard of Silver Seal Fitness?"

Hank butted in. "It's the finest sweat factory in Honolulu."

"How appetizing." Ava waved her pen and regarded the food to be tasted. "Oh, I'm remarkably familiar with the gym! I've worked with Jordan." She ducked her head confidentially to Hank. "I did their wedding."

Hank's smile curled downward. "I missed that event. The photos were good."

Conner nodded effusively. "We're the island's foremost fitness center and we're on local access TV."

Ava noted Hank's response to Jordan and Kirk's wedding photos. "Okay, that explains the variety of foods Sky and Conner have requested."

Hank sighed. "Oh yeah, we've got your vegans, we've got your health nuts, and then we have the people who come to events like locust to a field. We are an all-American family."

****

Hank extended the claim check to the valet and turned, smiling at Ava. "Will I see you at your usual place for pork and ginger meatballs? No wedding talk?"

Ava slanted Hank a smirk. "What did you say about the American League?"

Hank looked at Sky and Conner a few steps away. He lowered his voice and leaned toward Ava. "You heard me. But then, I'm not a baseball fan. I'd hate for that to come between us."

"That's okay, Hank, I'm a multi-faceted person." She tapped a nail on the center of his chest. "This is an island. You like water? How long can you hold your breath?"

Hank shrugged and took in the island ambiance. With a wave of his hand, he replied. "You realize I've been in the desert for the last ten years. He patted his trim midsection. "I know I float."

Ava nodded her head slowly. "You float, huh? We'll start with snorkeling."

Hank's car arrived, and he wondered if her spark was a wedding sales pitch or the beginning of something better.

****

Early the next morning, Hank sat at Kirk and Jordan's kitchen counter. "Why didn't you tell me Ava did your wedding?"

Kirk and Jordan stopped stirring their coffee and looked at each other. Kirk shrugged. Jordan grinned. "I think that's how Sky found her. I've used her for big events at the gym. Why? Is this good or bad news?" Jordan made one of those 'I Love Lucy' guilty faces.

Hank drew in a deep whiff of steaming coffee. "Oh, it's all good…"

Kirk slid a plate of fruit toward Hank. "She put our little wedding together on the run. Hell, you were overseas, we didn't have many guests. What's the deal, Teflon?"

"You know, Romeo, all this time I've been looking forward to more than flying…" Hank put down his coffee. "Well, I would have appreciated a heads up." He glanced at Kirk. "I know I was the one who told you to step up…" Hank gestured from Kirk to Jordan. "All these months I've been negotiating this wedding, I could have been cultivating more of…"

"What?" Kirk's hands went up. "Do I look like a… a matchmaker?"

"Of a friendship?" Jordan grinned at Hank over her pineapple spear and nudged her husband. "Maybe, Kirk, you could have put in a good word for him. You know, to make up for jumping in front of Teflon and proposing to me?"

Kirk barked out a laugh. "Hah! Should I warn the women of a certain age Teflon has landed, and their virtues are in danger?"

****

Hank thought about the passions he'd cultivated in his lifetime. Family and flying had always stirred his heart. Looking forward to retirement without someone to share it with loomed larger than before. He didn't need a Hawaiian meme to tell him it was another day in paradise when Hank strolled into The Dugout—the friendly and dark sports bar.

Hatless today, Ava held court in her usual seat as she sipped a fizzy cocktail. She spun on the barstool as Hank's baritone greeted Morty behind the bar. Today Hank recognized Ava's smile was warmer than yesterday's. *Don't fuck this up, General.* "Morty, take it easy on me. Start with a vodka Collins." It was easy to grin at the woman beside him.

She stirred her almost empty drink and returned his smile. "Good morning, Hank."

He checked his watch with a wink. "I believe it's almost noon, ma'am. How about a refill?" He gestured to her glass.

She nodded at Morty. "Don't be cheap with the limes this time."

Hank watched Morty ply his trade. Ava's drink was deceptively mild, a standard Shirley Temple with three lime wedges. As their glasses were set before them. He chuckled. "That's how you stay so clear-headed." They toasted and began sipping as Hank perused the bar's menu. "What's good?"

Morty moved to the other end of the bar and Ava tipped her head toward Hank and put her left hand over her mouth confidentially. He noticed she wore a bright gold leaf ring on her left hand. "What's good is the restaurant next door. Don't tell Morty I'm just here for the grenadine and limes."

Hank breathed a smile of confidence. They watched the array of TVs on the wall as they sipped and debated the sportsmanship of golf. Neither of them would be caught on the links. "So, ready for some real island food?"

Hank drew back. "You're not going to make me dig a pit for a pig, are you?"

When she shook her head, her blonde bob danced delightfully. "After so many years in the desert, I hope you still have a taste for seafood."

"I'm a chowhound. As long as I know what I'm eating, I'm game if you are." Hank finished his drink, peeled cash off his money clip, and they stepped into the bright sunshine. Hank extended his elbow as they plowed through the tourist-crowded sidewalk.

"Hank, you're retired, right?"

"Do I need my DDF 214?" His head was on a swivel, taking in the sights and sounds of the mélange of visitors.

Ava stopped walking, and he jerked to a stop. "No, we're on island time now. Relax."

"It's a hard habit to break." Hank nodded at the tourists. "You see people, I see troops lollygagging."

Ava patted his forearm. "Well, let me give you a crash course in constructive lollygagging." On her left arm, he noticed sunlight glinted off a bracelet of gold leaves that matched her ring.

Hank's lips curled mischievously. "Okay."

****

Enjoying his opah blackened Cajun style, Hank fluffed his macaroni salad with a fork and squinted. "Is this potato in my macaroni salad?"

Ava nodded. "Old family recipe, pretty simple, macaroni, hard-boiled eggs, potatoes, and mayo. We multitask here."

Hank surveilled the fork full. "Nothing Julia Child ever taught me."

Ava put down her utensils. "You've studied with Julia Child?"

"In a manner of speaking. Have you ever eaten MREs?"

Her answer was clipped. "Nope."

He grinned as he chewed. "Well, a man in the desert needs some respite. I learned to cook via YouTube. Julia was patient with me. Of course, I wore out a few mouse batteries, replaying her recipes."

"How could you possibly cook? Didn't you live in a tent?"

"The troops did. I had a Class-C RV as the ranking officer's quarters."

Ava made a simpering grimace. "In that heat?"

"Yeah, I cooked outside a lot." Hank watched Ava's responses to military life. "You don't have close family who served, do you?"

She shook her head. "My dad was in early Vietnam. He didn't talk about it."

Hank chewed thoughtfully. "Yeah, that was a rough one."

"Other than him, not really."

Hank saw their conversation darken. *Great, war talk at lunch.* "So, I used to have dinners monthly for my officers. We ate under the camo tent over my place. It wasn't easy cooking on a three-burner stove. Actually, only two worked, but I managed."

Ava sat fascinated. "I'm amazed. I wish my kitchen was three times the size. I'd kill for a double oven."

Kill for a double oven. Okay. "What do you like to cook?"

She pointed her fork at his dish. "I cook Cajun, and I should have warned you I can do a better blackened fish than any place on this island. Plus, my pineapple bread pudding is a gut buster with the rum sauce."

Hank sat back and shook his head. "I challenge you to a bake-off. Nobody turned down my Um Ali bread pudding with pistachios when I could get them." *I'm challenging my event planner to a bake-off? Have I left my nuts in Afghanistan? No, I have veritably lost my damn mind.*

Ava looked at her watch. "Oh, now you've done it. We have to have a bake-off. We need impartial judges…"

Judges? I know I have to put myself out there and talk to a bunch of different strangers and hope the conversations are long enough to get to a fair image of the other person. "I don't have more than the basics. I need to make a kitchen haul."

With speedy regard to their near-empty plates, Ava nodded. "Have I got a place to take you."

I bet you do…

****

Ava had to shake her head as she unlocked her car door for Hank. Twenty-four hours ago, she thought he was tailing her. Now he felt like a friend. A great part of that was connecting their history of emails for Sky's wedding. *This man is far more down to earth in the flesh. And the flesh I can see is fine.* He walked with an economy of graceful movement. His ready smile showed itself like punctuation.

When was the last time I gave a tinker's damn about a guy? Too damn long ago.

****

Well, of course, her car smells delightfully like Ava. Hank buckled up in the tidy marine blue Mercedes wagon and drew in calming scents. *What is that?* Hank was one part disconcerted that he wasn't driving and one part happy to have Ava navigate through 'paradise' and the vacationing crazies. They sat back, comfortable enough with each other to listen to a seventies radio station. Hank watched her right and left turns, committing the route to memory as Ava tapped a nail in tune with Heart's Barracuda. Keyed up by the nutcases trying to play bumper cars, he did the 'bliss breath' thing and smiled.

"Is this traffic crazy making or what?" Ava stopped at an intersection as Hank drew in a deep breath through his mouth.

"You handle it pretty well. It doesn't look like there are many back roads." Hank resettled in the seat and prepared for her navigating the parking lot.

When they did park and get out of the car, they behaved like any couple who shopped together for thirty years. Ava's hands flew in descriptions as she raved about the kitchen shop's collections. Hank walked in step with her, his head tilted in interested concentration. While he held the store's door open, he caught their sociable reflections. To the world, they looked like a couple.

Chapter Three

Hours later, Ava waited as Hank punched in his door code and threw open his condo door. Lumbering in with four huge shopping totes of spices, accessories, and bakeware, he dropped them on the kitchen floor. "If this was a fairytale, the squirrels would put things away."

Ava stood at the open refrigerator door. "News flash, you're on the twenty-fifth floor. No squirrels up here." She stepped aside and gestured. "We need another mission to fill your fridge."

Hank stood over Ava and took in her heady scent of cologne and a day's sunshine. "How about a happy-hour mission on the lanai?"

****

It was almost too easy to talk with her. By his second Longboard beer, Hank knew she'd been deserted by her husband and reinvented herself as an event planner on the island. Her easy smile and open body language invited him to admit a few things about himself.

"So, Air Force lifer?" Her blue eyes sparkled with curiosity.

"That's me." Hank shifted in the chair and his attention momentarily drifted to a tourist helicopter flying above the hotels on Waikiki. "I was just getting to be a family man. I had a toddler daughter and a wife I loved. The world was temporarily at peace, and then I got a call from the hospital. My wife was dead, and my toddler was motherless."

Ava's hand flew to her mouth. "Oh, Hank, I'm so sorry for both of you."

Hank sighed deeply. "I didn't know what decision to make. All I'd ever wanted to do was be a fighter pilot. How was I going to do that with a toddler? Dory's younger sister, Sherry, came to live with us on base, which was an immense help. I kept flying and got to see my daughter grow." He dragged a hand through his hair.

Ava nodded. "I can see why you want the best for Sky."

"Then, 9/11 happened, and we went to war. Aunt Sherry married Bob and moved to Florida. I was no longer stationed stateside. Sherry insisted on taking Sky with her. That's how it stayed until Sky went to college." Ava nodded. "Sky and I have butted heads, but it's brought us closer. I thank Sherry and her husband; I was Uncle Dad."

Ava rose and strolled to the balcony railing. "You've got a beautiful view of the canal and the beach skyline." While she faced the horizon, her voice sobered. "I wish my marriage had been more… stable. Sheldon never wanted children. For all his attention, I could have hidden twins at the house."

"The guy was never home?" Hank joined her at the railing and looked at Ava's profile in the afternoon light. "How could a man not want to be home with you?" He watched her blush spread across her pleasant face.

Ava's smile turned rueful. "You never met Sheldon. His big love affair was with other people's money."

"I'm glad our circumstances have brought us here, now that I'm an old, retired General."

Ava turned to Hank and leaned on the lanai railing. "Old? Oh, no… you're still vital enough to enjoy island life." Her smile was saucy. "There's always corporations looking for men with your experience." She squelched a grin. "And plenty of women on this island, too."

Hank's brow cocked, and his tongue slowly ran over his bottom lip. *And here's to dealing with the whole courting process and all the second-guessing and confusion that comes with it.* "Oh, yeah? You think the resort will let me work off Sky's expenses as a cabana boy?"

Ava chuckled softly before she shook her head. "Nope. At the cost of this shindig, you'd be working for the next ten years. There's an old saying, do what you love and…"

"…You never work a day of your life." Both of them leaned on the railing and listened to the distant sound of waves and vacationers twenty-five floors below.

On the nearby sports field, the softball team dropped their bags and warmed up for their game. "Oh, look, free entertainment, if you like softball."

Hank rubbed at the bridge of his nose. "Who, me? I was thinking about beginning the siesta habit."

Ava straightened her posture and tucked breeze-blown hair behind her ear. "I guess that's my cue to shuffle back to work."

Hank checked his watch. "If you're so inclined, they're doing fireworks tonight. I'll head out to the store and grab some grub, and you're welcome to come and watch the fireworks with me."

"Ooh, fireworks. Sure! What can I bring?"

"Your appetite and your good company." *So is tonight the night I ask myself if this is going anywhere? To see if she likes me and if I like her? Or am I playing the hand the airport dealt and like the idea of how we met? What am I supposed to do?* All the Google searches in the world couldn't argue with the idea of meeting woman where they're doing what they love. Hank loved travel, so why not get to know Ava Hansen?

* * * *

My good company. Ava blinked as she rode the elevator down. *What am I doing? He's the father of one of my brides. I can't think like this. We're just two new friends having dinner.*

When Sky contacted her and explained the long-distance situation, Ava thought of her client as 'the General.' She had expected a by-the-book, my-way-or-the-highway kind of guy. Every email was to the point unless it was about something Sky wanted. Then she read his enthusiasm at giving his daughter the wedding of her dreams.

When she watched him with the engaged couple, he reminded her of chocolate-covered cherries. The kind of candy that lulls you into eating the entire box, then you regret it when you realize it's sugar free.

As the fit and generally secure blonde in her late fifties settled into her car, she adjusted the rear-view mirror and looked at her cheeks. *Yes, he made me rosy and giggly.* And what's wrong with a divorcée blushing?

Regardless of the closet full of colorful clothing, Ava made a direct line to her favorite small boutique and chose something swingy and breezy, something soft. Picking up a perfume tester, she sniffed under the watchful eye of the woman half her age. "What's this?" Ava's brows rose at the smoky floral.

As the clerk wrapped her outfit in tissue, her smile grew sultry. "They call it a body incense… fruits, plants, woods, and that note of smoke. It smolders, doesn't it?"

"I'll take one." Ava plucked the small black box from the wicker bowl and swallowed hard at the implications.

****

Hank sucked in the equivalent of a sustained scream when he saw the Honolulu grocery prices. *Over nine dollars for a bag of salad? Jeesh. From now on, I do my shopping at the PX. Okay, kid, batter up.* As he pushed the cart through, he grabbed fish, shrimp, fresh fruit, and that ridiculous bag of spring mix. *Red wine? White wine? Rosé? Oh, hell,* he put a cardboard case in his trolley and mixed in his selection. He grabbed Lillet, and a variety of wines to be enjoyed with their meal, all the way to a brooding port.

Recipes bombarded him as he drove home. It helped keep his mind off what he was doing. *Am I romancing this woman?* Naw. *Yeah, I kind of am.*

Once Hank was home, he looked around the stark condo. It looked okay when he arrived the other day. Now, with the prospect of a woman in his 'place' it looked like a freshly painted and staged model unit with absolutely no charm. *Have I got to work on that? Yeah.*

The most attractive things in the kitchen were the batik Honu and hibiscus dishtowels draped over the top cabinet doors. He set up the new wine rack in the dining room and then moved it beside the sound system in the living room on the bar.

As Hank threw together the shrimp remoulade pasta salad, he blinked hard. Ava had bragged she might be the best Cajun cook on the island, and he trod on her ground. *Ah, here I go, into the breach.*

Showered, shaved, and casually dressed, he heard his doorbell. *Is Ava early?* Hank opened the door to the woman he had casually dated years ago, Jordan Roman.

"Oh!" Jordan's bright eyes widened before she stepped into the condo. She gave him a long once-over and her brows rose.

"Oh?" Hank regarded himself. "Can't a guy dress nice?" He stepped back and gestured Jordan into the foyer.

She peeked around the corner and giggled at the ingredients spread across the open kitchen. "Am I intruding?"

Hank looked at the clock and shook his head. "Only if you're here at seven when my guest arrives."

"Guest? Nice." Jordan swallowed her smile and glanced at the minimally fleshed-out apartment.

"Like the housewarming plant?" Hank gestured to the welcome home gift from the condo's management office. The dish garden featured the usual low wide ceramic bowl with a single peace lily, pothos, and peperomia. "Enjoy it now, I'll most likely kill it." Hank strolled to the beverage cooler under the small bar and offered her a bottle of water.

Jordan waved off the bottle and waggled her brows. "All you need is an aromatherapy diffuser, and this will be a real smash pad."

Hank cocked a look at her. "That could work. I asked Ava, the event planner, over for the fireworks. I can tune in the music on the radio, right?"

Jordan turned and peered at him. "Ah, Ava!" She ambled around the buffet-style table set and waiting for food.

Hank's gaze drifted to the lanai with the double chaise and side tables set with candles. "Are the candles too much?"

Jordan folded her arms over her chest and smirked. "Nope, it's exactly how I'd like it." They grinned at each other, and she extended her hand to his forearm. "I heard the kids were busy tonight, so I came down to ask if you wanted to come up for… dinner and the fireworks, but I see you work fast."

"Work fast? Kirk taught me to speak up. Say a prayer I didn't read her wrong, that I'm not being reckless."

"Wrong? You reckless? No, on either of those things. Ava is a great gal, and I don't think she's seeing anyone. I'll bug out and get back upstairs." Jordan walked out to the lanai and looked up a few floors, where Kirk leaned over the railing with two glasses of sangria. She blew a kiss, waved, and looked back at Hank. "My cocktail awaits, so you have a nice night."

The brief time Jordan was there was enough to crack Hank's confidence. As Jordan pecked a friendly kiss on his cheek in parting, he shook off the feeling of uncertainty and shored up his swagger. Then he set up a casual playlist of oldies. *Hope she likes oldies in music and men.*

****

Ava stood at Hank's door, keenly aware of the scent of her new perfume. The pineapple prickled her palm and the decorative clip in her hair slipped precariously. She stuck the pineapple between her knees and re-twisted her hair to clip it tighter. That was the inconvenient moment when Hank's door opened.

Hank smiled as she righted herself and caught the pineapple. "I didn't even ring the door."

Hank held out his phone. "It's my new security doorbell."

"I'll remember that…" Her words tapered off in embarrassment. "Here, my welcome gift to you. My southern heritage has a custom of bringing a pineapple to a new homeowner."

Hank smiled and welcomed her into his home. "Should we eat it tonight?" He thumped it. "Is it ripe?"

"Oh, yes, smell it. It's fruity." Ava spied the incredibly tidy kitchen. "Have you started cooking yet? The table is beautiful."

Hank threw the apron strap over his head and tied it around his waist. "Remember that RV? This place is an embarrassment of space in comparison. When you're cooking in an RV, you learn to clean as you go… May I offer you a glass of wine?"

"If you'll join me." She followed him to the small bar in the living room. There was a new wine rack, and it was full. "You've shopped since I was here last."

Hank narrowed his gaze. "Do you know how much they want for a bag of salad? I'm going to container farm on my lanai. I'll make a fortune selling what I don't eat." Hank removed the chilled Lillet bottle and searched for the corkscrew. "Good thing this bottle is screw off. I've misplaced the corkscrew." She nodded at the screw-off top. Noticing the beads of perspiration on his freshly shaven upper lip, she thought, *Is he nervous?* He poured glasses and offered one to her.

Ava lifted her flute. "Here's to American enterprise." They touched glasses and took a drink of the wine.

"Care to keep me company while I fix the fish?"

Ava stood on the other side of the counter as Hank moved efficiently at first. "Missing something?"

Hank leaned on the counter. "They haven't delivered my crate with my cedar plank." He gusted out a heavy sigh, the size of his six-foot-three frame. "Now the fish will stick to the grill."

Ava swallowed her wine and raised a finger. "The pineapple, cut it lengthwise and use slices of pineapple as planks. Caramelize it, lay the fish on it, and cover it while we enjoy your first course."

Hank nodded, wielding a large cleaver over the fruit. Ava yelped. "Wait!"

"What?" He held back the shiny implement.

"Lop off the top and plant it. You'll grow your own."

Hank followed her pineapple dissection direction. "Just don't put the pot outside your front door."

"What, not enough light?"

She shook her head. "No, people will think you swing."

Hank frowned doubtfully. "They'll think I swing? That I swing pineapples?"

Ava's hand covered her mouth as she blushed. She looked around anywhere but at his smiling face. "You know 'swing.' As in couples together…" She shot a look toward where she thought the bedroom was.

"Is this an island thing?" Hank dropped the top in the sink.

"Oh, no. It's all over the internet." Ava stared determinedly into her drink.

Hank raised a brow. "You must visit some interesting sites."

She waved him off. "Our events are on TikTok. Some of the other things I see there are… doozies."

After Hank followed her advice about the cooking process, he covered the food to cook. He carried the bottle of Lillet in the wine chiller out to the lanai. "We have some time until the fireworks show. Let's relax." They did a little dance, like mating porcupines around the lanai seating. Hank took the chair and Ava stretched out on the large chaise. Hank picked up a pita chip and drew it through the dip. "I've never seen a dip like this, but it sounded good. The deli clerk said it was salty, creamy, fruity, and sweet."

Ava plucked a cracker from the tray and nodded. "Oh, welcome to island life and Hawaiian onion dip." She felt his scrutiny, and returned it. *He has great calves and that manspread of his looks nice… and packed.* She caught herself before he caught her. *Great, I am chewing like a cow.* She glanced in Hank's direction. *But we both are.* "This is very good."

The Motown playlist shifted, and Earth, Wind, and Fire slipped into a smooth tune. The conversation lulled as they snacked and sipped. When Ava read his awkwardness, she spoke up. "You must be so proud to go into business with your daughter's fiancé. The two of them are on such a stellar track."

Hank blushed. "Oh, you should have been here when she proposed being an artist. You can't pick what your kids will do." He swept another chip through the dip and hesitated. "I greased the wheels to get her into the Air Force Academy."

Ava's jaw dropped. "Seriously, Hank? Sky in the military?"

Hank nodded. "That was her response, too. I promised I'd visit her living in a box under the overpass as a portrait artist. She surprised the hell out of me." He shrugged. "It could so easily have gone the other way. The odds were not in her favor. My friends, the Romans, commissioned her to do a mural at the gym and it caught the right person's eye. She took off from there." He nodded. "It's all about who you know."

****

Ava fell back against the chaise. "Oh, please, don't I know that." Hank's brow rose. "I'm thrilled to say I've met all the right people on this island."

Hank's shoulders relaxed as he nodded along with her story. "How did you end up here?"

"Oh, it was a couple of shows. Do you remember that cute comedy about the retired stunt man called *Shaken and Stirred?*"

Hank tilted his head at her question. "Remember, I was in the desert?"

"It was the cutest thing." Ava gushed, "The character's name was Torrance Mayne. A big heartthrob." She made air quotes. "His nickname was To' Mayne. You know the type, he had done stunts for Hawaiian Spy a decade ago, but he was done jumping off bridges. He stayed on the island and needed work, so they wrote this cute show about a stuntman turned TV chef. I was the chef behind the chef."

"How did you come out of this without owning a restaurant?"

"I never wanted to be nailed down. I like doing events. Besides, the star and his wife are good friends of mine. I do all their son's birthday parties."

Hank was in such a great mood as he walked to the kitchen he hummed along with the funky tunes from his playlist. He looked at the pineapple, perfectly caramelized, and retrieved the salmon from the fridge. He paid no mind to the stove's 'click' as he closed the oven door. Layering the salmon slices over the pineapple slabs, Hank slid them back into the oven. He glanced at the temperature, set the timer, and almost danced back out to Ava. "It shouldn't be long before our tantalizing dinner is ready. We've been drinking an apéritif wine. Hold on..." Hank slid open the unfamiliar kitchen drawers and found a corkscrew. He held it up. "Look what I found. Now I can offer you some white wine for the fish." He held the bottle and two fresh glasses aloft.

Ava swallowed the last sip and smiled. "Aren't you the connoisseur to have wine, by the course?" Hank opened the bottle and presented the cork.

Ava leaned conspiratorially. "I have no idea what I'm supposed to smell from this cork. That's why I employ a sommelier." She sniffed, smiled, and returned the cork. "Smells sweet to me."

The sky outside glowed with the deep purple sunset. Traffic signals and headlights became visible below. As they stood and watched the busy traffic, Ava turned to Hank. "Tell me about your dreams for Kingston Air."

Hank looked like he was going to speak and buried a smirk. "Well, the best thing about our licensing is, at my age, I can still fly. Commercial pilots age out at sixty-five."

Ava leaned back, as if to rate his age. "Oh, I wasn't aware of the age thing."

Hank nodded and went on. "First, I was going to name it Sky Air and Kirk Roman blew a raspberry and said, 'what else do you fly through than air?" He shook his head. "Then Conner suggested King-Con Air. I thought he'd suggest a logo with a giant ape. That wasn't dignified. So, being the majority stockholder, it's my name on the tail."

Ava raised her glass. "Branding is everything. At least they know who the boss is."

"I've been fortunate to have a silent partner who trusts me to know my stuff. The bank thinks he's big enough to give me credence…" Hank leaned on his forearm and watched the colors of the sunset wash over Ava's blonde hair and tanned complexion. He shook his head. "I'm sorry I'm giving you an investor pitch. I haven't had a pleasant night with a fascinating woman in too long to tally."

Ava tucked her chin and blushed. "I'll bet when you were the top dog you didn't meet too many women."

"You're right about that. And if I did, they were wives or subordinate officers." He watched her posture soften as she relaxed against the railing.

"So much better for me to welcome you to island life."

Before his thoughts could take him into embarrassing physical territory, the timer dinged. "Excuse me, I'll plate dinner." His gaze swept the empty dining room table and his lizard brain plotted. *I'd rather plate her.* The angel on his other shoulder warned. *Hank, don't do it, at least not tonight.*

The open oven door released no wave of heat. The tray of fish sat forlornly in a tepid oven. He ran his hand under the heating element inside. *Nada. Nothing.* As he heard the click clack of Ava's sandals behind him, he held up the tray. "How do you feel about salmon poke?"

Ava pointed a bright coral nail at his disaster. "Did you buy frozen sushi-grade salmon?"

Hank's brows knit. "Was I supposed to?"

Ava winced at the raw fish. "You didn't have to if you planned to cook it. But this fish, we need to cook. I'm guessing your oven is on the fritz?"

"You are correct."

"Let me help. I can do a pan-fried teriyaki to die for. Sit on the other side of the bar and let me work my magic."

Hank pouted as he set the pan down and untied his apron. "This was supposed to be my night to impress you with my hunter-gathering skills."

She stepped closer and when their hands glanced on the apron, time stood still. Hank's motor revved. He dropped the apron collar over Ava's head, and she patted his cheek. "Oh, you hunted just fine. I don't trust this brand of stove. You, I trust."

He leaned over the bar and watched her assemble what she needed. Neither knew where everything was. His new gear still cluttered the far counter.

"If you're putting me to work, I'll need that wine glass." Ava situated herself over a cutting board and chopped the pineapple. Hank retrieved their glasses and paused in handing hers over, seeing both her hands covered with caramelized pineapple. "Got a straw?"

Hank's smile evaporated. "No."

"Come closer. I don't bite, just hold it to my lips."

Hank put his glass down. Her cologne made a heady mix with the scents of the teriyaki. *How did the kitchen get so warm when the oven isn't?* Being within arm's length of her made his knees weak. He'd eat an MRE if he could stay within her orbit. When he held the glass to her coral lips, he nearly melted into her as the tip of her tongue darted into the glass. He liked it. Debating food over romance, Hank stepped back to watch her cook.

He leaned his elbow on the counter, smiling at her grace at managing the meal. "You're most likely thinking I planned this to get out of cooking."

She slanted a look at him. "If I hadn't heard about the RV with the twenty-one-inch oven, I might think that. But if I know a fellow foodie who finally has a full kitchen, your next phone call will be to the appliance repair tech.

Hank crossed his arms over his chest and shrugged. "I think I'll upgrade. I've been renting this out to one couple since I bought the place. I had it painted after they moved out, but seriously, it is time for a new kitchen."

Ava's gaze scanned the bottles of spices lined up like troops. His blonde sorcerer's apprentice uncapped and dashed bits of this and that into the saucepan for the glaze. Again, her tiny sliver of tongue darted to taste the edge of the spoon. She tilted her head, holding one hand under the hand with the spoon, and she offered it to Hank. "Does this have enough ginger?"

His hand slid under hers and as he bent over the spoon to taste, he caressed her soft skin. His lips sealed over the spoon, and they stood frozen in the moment. "Seems just right to me." He stroked her hand again. "Your skin feels like a fresh peach." Electricity sparked between them. They each jumped back.

"What was that?" Ava looked at him, bright-blue eyes aflash.

Hank buried a grin. "If my engineering education is correct, *you* are a live wire, Ms. Hansen." He watched her blush rise.

Ava steadied herself between his hip and the oven. "Oh, is this your bawdy humor? I like bawdy humor. It's so hard to find."

Hank took a step back, with a chuckle rising from his belly. He held up a hand. "I like you, Ava. I bet you're a swell gal."

She turned back to the saucepan and winked over her shoulder. "You may want to revise your opinion after you've tasted my teriyaki."

Hank swallowed another chuckle and shook his head. "I don't think so."

****

Dinner was wonderful. The night sky fell, and the radio played softly in the background as they claimed the two sides of the wide chaise. As the announcer welcomed tonight's listeners, the ground crew jumped the gun and the first explosion spread across the sky.

Ava startled with a giggle and surrendered to his strong arm, catching her to him. She cradled her wine glass and cuddled into him. "Umm, thank you, Mr. Fireworks Man."

At her nod, Hank slipped her glass from her fingers and set it with his on the side table. "Fireworks are just an accident waiting to happen."

All Ava heard in his words was seduction. *Would it be an accident to fall into his kiss?* She whispered, "What did Bob Ross say about happy accidents?"

Hank frowned as his gaze narrowed. "Is he a prior beau?"

"Oh, silly, you have been in the desert awhile." Ava giggled and hugged this teddy bear of a man. "He had a painting show and all his splatters became 'happy accidents.'"

A screaming spider of light flashed as they gazed into each other's eyes. They looked up and Ava gasped. "Wow."

Hank's attention riveted on her, and he kissed her cheek. "Yeah, wow."

She turned into his lips and her words came out in a breath. "Yeah, wow!" Ava tasted the ginger sauce in Hank's kiss. She watched his brown eyes darken. That old 'personal summer' flashed through her. Or was it him? Was he doing this to her? *I think it's him.*

****

The next morning, Hank stumbled around his condo, shellshocked. Somewhere in his brain, the silly happy song about being 'happy' played in his head. Had he walked Ava to her car in the garage and sent her home after a make-out session that ended long after the Waikiki fireworks? *Yes, I did. And to be honest, the lady gave as good as she received.*

Man, he hadn't tussled like that since high school. And how did it end? Pretty much like high school, except Hank walked Ava to her car in the garage downstairs. At least her parents weren't staring at them through curtains on her front porch.

After their last extended kiss, through her car's open window, Ava started her car and drove off. Before Hank took the elevator back upstairs, he realized the old guy on the second floor must have appointed himself the garage sentry. The old guy rocked, and gave Hank a thumbs up before the elevator doors closed.

Breathing deeply, Hank rode up twenty-five floors with his heart in his throat. When he got into his place, he stripped down and got into his shower. Hank closed his eyes and projected her over-kissed smile in his mind. Then he ran cold water and let out a frustrated growl.

Even before he got into bed, he regretted tomorrow's commitment to his best friend, Kirk Roman. He agreed to give the former SEAL a hand at his place, Silver Seal Fitness Club. He wasn't going to feel like working out in the morning. God knew he was experienced in putting troops through their paces, but what spandex-covered gym rats was he going to face at eight AM?

Chapter Four

From force of habit, Hank carried his PT clothes in his gym bag. He jogged up the steps to the front desk where the hyper-fit Kirk met him.

"You're not dressed out," Kirk reprimanded.

Hank barked back. "Per regulation, gym wear is for the gym only. Where's my locker?" He held up his gym bag.

"Learn to retire, General." Kirk dropped his chin. "We'll outfit you in Silver Seal gear for next time…if you're tough enough for next time."

Jordan Roman, the one who got away from Hank six years ago, watched from behind the front counter. "The class is bouncing off the walls downstairs while you two are flapping your gums." She pulled two towels from under the counter and tossed them to Hank. "How was your date last night?"

Kirk froze in place. "You had a date?"

Hank narrowed his gaze as he looked at the clock. "Romeo, we better get a move on."

As Kirk and Hank headed downstairs, Hank shot a look at his friend. "Has she always been this nosy?"

Kirk winked. "I like it, since you never tell me anything."

Hank shook his head. "So, your classes, are they always this out of control? I thought you knew how to lead your troops?"

They came to the bottom of the steps, where the two locker rooms flanked the mat room. Hanks's eyes widened at the area full of five-year-olds currently causing mayhem. They bounced and rolled on the blue mats in a cacophony of screeches that threatened to decalcify his spine. Hank turned to Kirk. "What…?"

Kirk clamped a hand on his shoulder and pushed him toward the locker room. "Welcome to the world of civilian commercial demand." He tapped his watch. "I'm timing you. Class at 0805."

****

Kirk checked off the children's names as Hank collected permission slips for the exercise class, Keiki Commotion. Hank turned his back to the fidgeting kids. "You're not leaving me with them, are you?"

Kirk accepted the forms and slid them onto the clipboard. "Of course not, you're not trained for this… yet. By the end of the week, you'll be doing this in your sleep." Kirk took a step closer. "By the way, you did use protection, right? Otherwise, these arrive." He motioned to the kids shattering Hank's nerves.

"None of your business." Hank turned away, muttering, "In my nightmares, I'll be here next week." He turned back to Kirk and hissed. "How young do you think my date was?" Kirk shrugged.

But Hank's smile was Pepsodent bright as he faced the keiki. The little girls clamored for his attention and did cartwheels and somersaults. The boys wrestled like they were WWF recruits.

Kirk clapped sharply, and the kids stood stunned in place. "Everyone, find a dot on the mat. That's your dot." Half the kids jumped to the dot nearest them. A few ambled to find a dot near a friend. One little girl wandered around looking for a dot in the back row. "Trinity, where's your dot?"

The little blonde with a riot of curls chewed her forefinger. "Guess what, Mr. Roman?"

Kirk stood before his favorite little star-child, crouching to her eye to eye. "I couldn't in a million years. What?"

"Danny took my dot." She pointed the wet finger to a space.

Kirk turned to Danny. "Danny?"

Danny pulled down the neck of his tank top to reveal the red dot. With fists shaking at his side, Danny proclaimed, "I AM IRON MAN!"

Kirk peeled a new dot from the bottom of his clipboard and placed it where Trinity stood. "Okay, Mr. Stark, you can keep that dot." Kirk dropped the clipboard on the counter and cued the energetic exercise music. Kirk nodded and whispered to Hank. "Get your ass over here, next to me." When his reluctant friend was outside arm's length, Kirk bellowed, "Who's a star?"

The kids immediately screamed. Hank shuddered. Standing tall, they explosively jumped into the air, arms, and legs aloft. It was a room of flying 'X's. At the height of their jumps, the room shook with juvenile screeches. "I'm a STAR!"

Kirk bellowed. "Again!" Hank shot a wincing look at the former SEAL. "You're not a star? Why aren't you a star?" Hank became a star.

After the kids split Hank's eardrums. Kirk growled and posed like a bear. "Bear Crawls."

Danny jumped up and down. "Pick me, pick me, I want to be the big bear!"

Kirk motioned his troublemaker up to the front to demonstrate the position. With palms and feet flat on the floor, the boy arched his back, so he looked like a bear. "Hank, fall in last. Line up kids, two lines."

Trinity hung back, seeking Hank's attention by pulling on the hem of his shorts. He diverted from his pack and dropped to one knee. "What's up, sweetie?"

"I don't want to put my hands on the mat."

"Why not? Does it hurt?"

Her shoulders rose and fell as she twisted and ducked her head. "Floors are nasty."

Hank drew in a deep breath, playing with a response. "This isn't a floor." He tapped the mat. "This is made to roll and play on. Go ahead."

Trinity lowered her head and put her fists on her tiny hips. "Really? Okay." Trinity fell into line with her half of the class, and Danny was the first bear to lead the race.

Kirk gestured to Hank. "Who can 'roar' the loudest?" As two lines of kids bear-walked the length of the room, thundering and growling, Hank reminded himself to thank the Creator that Ava couldn't get pregnant, or so she intimated to him.

****

Sky worked out on a rowing machine. At an abrupt noise, she turned to Jordan. "What is that?" The sound shook the floor.

Jordan smiled and switched the feed on the televisions in Sky's area. "That is the sound of kids who don't play outside all week. Watch this." Sky stopped rowing, watching Hank and Kirk. When her dad went on one knee to the little girl, her heart began to melt. *Why? Why does he have to be so cute? Any woman from what, five, six, years of age falls under his spell.* She watched him play alongside the kids.

Jordan took time from the front desk and brought Sky a clean towel. Jordan leaned against the next machine and bit her bottom lip. "Did you know he had a date last night?"

"Date?" Sky gawked. "Daddy… had a… date?

Jordan shrugged. "I used to date him."

"Yeah, but that was ages ago when he was younger."

Jordan flinched and let that pass. They looked up at the monitor. Kirk and Hank behaved like first graders, lost in playful abandon.

"He is going to be so adorable when you have kids. No rush from me…" Jordan pushed away from the machine and scanned the room for anyone who needed her.

Sky wiped down her rowing equipment. "Within three months, that big goof is going to be a hotshot CEO and all the women will be circling him." She looked at her watch. "I'm heading to the wedding planner's office; she's got something neat to show me. See you at Dad's tonight. We're bringing dinner. His oven is kaput."

****

Hank showered after the session with the kids. When he stepped out of the locker room, he saw Kirk acting too casual to be casually 'there'. "What's on your mind, Romeo?"

Kirk's smile widened and went serious. "Got a minute, Teflon?" Kirk motioned to his office and Hank fell into step with him.

"Got a few, but I'm still getting moved in." Hank caught his image in a mirror and spiked his hair. Kirk held out a bottled water, and he accepted it. "It's been a while since I've been here in the principal's office."

Kirk's brows rose as he got situated in his chair and leaned back, one foot on an open bottom drawer. "You all equipped for … romance, Teflon?"

Hank blanched at the question. "Hey, I've been getting ready since before I packed my kit overseas. Have you spent the last five years reading how to satisfy women after fifty?" He gestured to Kirk. Need pointers, or are you solid?"

Kirk coughed a laugh and pointed upward. "You see Jordan's still smiling, right? I'm covered."

Hank looked upward and shrugged. "The squirrelly things I read were the exercises for men, but I was fascinated when I learned Tantric sex is more popular with guys our age."

"Yeah, seven hours of sex. Sting just didn't mention that included the foreplay of dinner and a movie."

"No, no, it's more… I used it to lower my blood pressure…"

"You did what?" Kirk sat up abruptly.

"I don't have to tell you about a link between the effects of relaxation, meditation, and spirituality with total health. What do you think I did alone at night, knit?" Hank folded his arms over his chest and grinned. "That got you curious now, Romeo, didn't it? I've got the savvy. Now all I need is the right woman for the relationship."

****

Ava bustled into her office centrally located in the Waialae Corridor. Being positioned between the University of Hawaii and Kahala Mall made it easy to access the H1 Freeway. She pushed through the front door and bellowed, "Mano!"

The man in the back cubicle rose from his chair. "Ms. Hansen. Good to have you back."

She dropped her packages on the desk. "Where have you been? I've been back for two days. Did you sign for three crates from Las Vegas?"

Mano picked up his tablet and scrolled, shaking his head. "One big skid arrived from Jimmy Choo. The bill of lading says forty-eight pieces at $3,700.00 each." He whistled and shook his head. "You bought diamond sneakers? Are they real diamonds?"

Ava snatched the tablet from him. "I'm not insane. I didn't buy diamond sneakers." *But I did buy two pairs of Louboutins, glad they weren't delivered here.* "We don't have any athletic-themed events this month."

Mano ran through the calendar. "Nothing until the University homecoming, and they wouldn't put out $178,000.00 for sneakers."

"I hope I didn't either. That check will bounce." Ava pulled at the scarf around her neck. "Let me see that bill of lading."

Both inspected the fine print and the delivery address of the suite next door. Mano shook his head. "I've got to stop hiring these cousins of mine. They'll sign for anything."

"Well, I'm not out anything. Why don't you go next door and tell them we have their ridiculous shoes?" Ava calmed with the knowledge the error was easily handled at no expense to her. She put a hand on Mano's forearm before he left. "I want you to be on the lookout for those three crates from Las Vegas. I scored the same cake video system as Disney Weddings. I'll be the singular event planner in all of Hawaii with these projectors." She pulled out her phone and played a short scene of a horse-drawn carriage letting a bride off on the top of the tall cake.

Mano scratched his head. "Does it do anything else?"

Ava rolled her eyes. "No. It doesn't need to do anything else. Do you have any idea how many brides will beat a path to my door for this?"

"Nothing has arrived other than diamond sneakers."

****

Ava buzzed Sky into the foyer from her office. "Hello, Sky! Come back here. I want to show you something I found for your wedding cake. If you want this, you'll be the first bride on the island to have this."

Sky took a seat as Ava cued up the video. The demo tape began at the bottom of the cake with six white mice and a pumpkin. With a magical swirl of stars, they became Cinderella's carriage. The fairy godmother waved a wand over a waif and turned her into a magnificent bride. Once in the carriage, the video projected up the sides of the cake to arrive at the castle where her prince awaited. "The best part is, we can make any type of video. We can have airplanes and art, whatever you want."

Sky was spellbound. "This is a dream! We can brand our business and tell our story."

Ava nodded excitedly. "I'm expecting delivery any day now. Meanwhile, we can sit down and choose the images."

Sky pulled up short. "How much will this cost us?"

Ava negated her worry with a wave of her hand. "You're the first. I'll give you a deal. The same price as the cake you were looking at, only the cake will be white on white."

Sky gasped. "It's a deal! This is phenomenal! Thank you for thinking of us."

****

After Sky left, the office was a little too quiet. Mano had gone next door before Sky arrived and he wasn't back yet. Ava walked through the warehouse full of folding chairs, tables, and organized event decorations. It was quiet except for running water. Mano stood at the safety sink filled with wet and blood-stained paper towels, dabbing at his swollen nose.

Ava gasped. "What happened?"

Mano did exactly the wrong thing to treat a bloody nose. He held his head back and squeezed his nostrils.

"No, no, no! Don't do that!" Ava chastised. "It's like this." She repositioned his fingers to hold pressure just below the bridge of his nose and bent his head forward. "You swallow all that blood and soon you'll be puking as well as bleeding." Mano groaned. "Did this come on suddenly?"

Mano's gaze narrowed as his face turned sinister. "It happened when I informed the lolo guy next door that we had his sneakers. While I was there, I saw our three crates, and I told him, there's been a mistake, brah. They delivered our stuff to you and your stuff to us. So, he hit me!"

Ava pulled herself up to her full five-foot-seven inches and shook her head. "We'll just see about that!" She started to march for the door, and Mano put an arm out to stop her.

"No, no place for a wahine. I think I got a look at crates of guns. That's why I got slugged. Whatever's going on, they look like company men."

"'Company?'" Ava frowned.

"Company, you know, the local gangsters. The Chinese Triad. They looked Triad to me."

She reached for the phone in her pocket. "I'm calling the police."

"No!" His emphatic word echoed in the warehouse. "You call the police on the Triad, and somebody will be planning our funeral."

Ava huffed out a breath. "This had to have been some underling who's misrepresenting his boss. I'm going to find out who owns that warehouse and speak to the owner of record. We'll get this straightened out." She stared at the empty cage where high-dollar items were locked. "Move those damn shoes into that cage and drop the blinds around it. I don't want anyone seeing what we have." She patted Mano's back and clipped to her office.

****

Ava dialed the number she'd finally won after several irritating phone calls. The owner of the property next door was certainly secretive. The telephone was answered curtly by a deep and heavily accented voice. "Most Acclaimed Imports."

"What?"

The annoyed receptionist repeated, "Most Acclaimed."

"I need to speak to Mr. Huang."

"Which Mr. Huang?"

"Whichever Huang owns the warehouse near the H1." The person on the line hung up. Ava redialed. "Mr. Huang, please." Another hang-up. Ava pressed redial as she reined in a flurry of curses. She got the company answering machine. "I'm calling for Peng Huang. This is Ava Hansen from Hau'oli Events. My company is next door to yours. Our warehouses are separated by a wall. It seems someone delivered a pallet of shoes to us that was meant for you and delivered three crates to you that were meant for us. Let's be hoa noho and exchange these items with a minimum of fuss. I have to tell you..."

49

The recorder ended, and she shook her head and redialed. The answering machine replied. "The mailbox for this number is full." Click. *What incredible nerve.*

Mano popped his head into her office, waving a finger. "Don't go there." By this time, he sported two black eyes and a swollen nose.

"I want you to go to the Emergency Room and get checked. I need a report for the authorities." Ava glanced at her watch. It was almost 5:00. "I'll lock up and set the alarm since I'm sitting on a gold mine. Maybe we'll get a polite answer in the morning."

Mano shook his head. "When pigs fly."

****

Bright and early the next morning, Ava bounded into the office feeling accomplished despite yesterday's disaster of an afternoon. The City of Honolulu had made its choice for the producer of this year's Mrs. Hawaii contest. Hau'Oli/She Lives Aloha Events, her company won the contract. *This will open a whole new revenue stream.* She knew it was in no small part because of her experience with television. *I've got to get those three projection sets back. I'll need every one of them.*

Mano barreled through the warehouse door to the front office. "We've been cleaned out! Everything is gone down to the pallet jack. Bastards!"

Ava leapt to her feet. "What?"

Mano stood before her desk; his breathing hitched. "Everything is gone except the mice!"

Ava ran to the warehouse door, and despite her disbelief, saw Mano was correct. The crooks had even swept the floor and taken the broom. How did something so outrageous throw her into a laughing fit? Mano stood back from her. She paced the perimeter of the one hundred and forty-four square feet of clean concrete in the cage. She turned to Mano. "Call the police. I'll call the insurance company."

50

****

She was handed a business card by Detective Li, a fifty-something world-weary type who reminded her of an Asian Columbo if Columbo wore a rumpled Aloha shirt. He looked up at her through sorrowful, dark eyes. At that moment, Ava saw only a basset hound. "You know you share this building with an alleged front for the Triad?"

Ava glanced up at Mano and she saw Li catch the look. His expression grew suspicious. "As of yesterday, we wondered about that. I told you, Mano had a run-in with one of their enforcers." She gestured to Mano's abused face.

Li's brow rose. "And that was over … the shoes?"

Li stretched Ava's patience. "That was over confused deliveries as I explained."

As the detective listened, he ran a hand over his face, rubbing in the area of Mano's injuries. "It looks like they fixed your nose?" Li nodded to Mano's split lip and bruises. "If that's the worst of it, you're lucky."

Ava felt as explosive as Mauna Loa. "Lucky? I'm wiped out. I'm grateful Mano was not permanently hurt." She cast her assistant a sympathetic glance. "But you do understand I have been robbed of easily $200,000.00 worth of inventory. What are you going to do about recovering my property?"

Li huffed a breath. "It looks like it was an inside job to me."

Ava spewed a volcanic response. "What?"

Detective Li paced away from her, looking at the clean floor. "You showed me the security settings. No one tampered with anything. Dock doors didn't go up and down. Your alarm didn't go off." He worked his jaw and sniffed. "Your security system only has a camera outside at the loading dock. You don't have one in here."

Ava's fists released explosively. "I trust my employees. Mano and I are the only two key and code holders. Anyone else, I set a temporary one, and then it reverts."

Detective Li nodded. "Right, it looks like an inside job." He stared up at the rafters. "Nobody came through the roof. Well, I'll file my report and let forensics know they have a clean place to work."

Ava considered his grin rather grim. "Right, sure."

He bobbled his pen at her. "Get a different system, Ms. Hansen. Better yet, if I were you, I'd move." He pointed next door and shook his head.

****

Right before lunchtime, while Ava was taking two aspirin, Hank and Sky arrived in tremendous moods. Before they could greet each other, Sky smiled effusively. "Daddy thinks the cake idea is cool." She vibrated youthful enthusiasm. Hank's friendly gaze simmered as if he wanted to kiss her cheek, or more.

Their zeal failed to vibrate over to Ava, who sat at her desk massaging her temples.

Hank drew closer as the warehouse door slammed shut. "Ava, are you okay?"

Mano ambled in looking like a recent accident victim. His voice was nasal as he asked, "What do you want me to do now, Ms. Hansen?"

Ava dropped her head. "Go home, Mano," she instructed wearily. "Get comfortable and put ice on your face. We're dead in the water." Mano gave a hang-dog nod and left.

"Welcome to my nightmare." She gestured for Hank and Sky to sit. "I am fortunate to offer you the last two chairs in the building. Beware, at any moment, Mano or I will make them disappear."

Hank leaned forward, his folded hands between his knees. "Say what?"

Ava clamped down on the temptation of tears at his sympathetic tone. "I've been robbed. If it was *in* the warehouse, it's gone now."

Sky gasped. "It's a good thing your cake projectors hadn't arrived. I was telling Daddy about them…"

Ava's gaze threw laser beams at the common wall between her and her neighbor. "About those cake projectors." She watched the father and daughter exchange concerned looks. "Perhaps you noticed Mano looked as if he'd gone two rounds with Mike Tyson?" They nodded. "Five minutes after the Detective walked the scene, he confirmed what Mano thought." She hooked a thumb next door. "They're Triad. Of course, on the heels of announcing that, he accused us of stealing our property, said it was an inside job."

Hank groaned. "Meaning the insurance won't pay you."

Ava sighed heavily. "Correct." The volume of tears she'd held all morning rained down as she hid behind fisted hands. She blubbered. "I'll never be insurable again. I'm finished."

****

Hank had seen a career's worth of civilians experiencing a total loss from plundering battles. Now, in civilian life, it was more than catastrophic. Now, the only resource he had was a shoulder to cry on and his embrace. Once he had her out of the chair, she melted against him, and her quivering slowed to a sob. He patted her head. "Come on, Sunshine."

Sky's eyes went round, and she silently mouthed "Sunshine?" as she pulled tissues out of the box on the desk.

Hank nodded as he soothed Ava. Sky volunteered, "There has to be something we can do… Conner's brother knows people."

Ava's head came up from Hank's chest. "'Knows people?' What kind of people?"

Hank patted her shoulder. "Let's take a walk in the back. We'll walk this off while we think…" The tail end of Hank's words echoed against empty concrete walls.

Sky pointed to a chain-link cage, the door gaping open with a missing padlock. "What was there?"

Ava smirked. "I kept high-dollar items there."

Hank broke away from Ava's embrace and paced the twelve-by-twelve-foot area. "What was in here last night?"

"$178,000.00 of the most ridiculous shoes you've ever seen. It's a long story."

Hank crouched at the wall and ran his hand up a narrow seam in the concrete blocks. "Was this building one tenant before you moved it?"

Ava stood, perturbed. "It's been two tenants for six years."

Hank rose and turned to Ava, rubbing damp grit between his fingers. "I'll tell you how they got in without disturbing your alarm. They cut through the concrete block." He stood back and pointed to the clean seam cut across the staggered block. "The detective didn't catch this?" Hank rubbed his fingers together to dissipate the damp concrete dust.

Ava growled. "The detective appeared to be afraid of my neighbors, the Triad. He advised me to move."

Hank struck a commanding pose. "Move? Then they just do the same thing to the next tenant. What if the next place you move has some other gangsters?" He crossed the distance to her and held her close. "Sky, honey, you take the car and go home. Ava and I are going to look at security equipment."

CHAPTER FIVE

Ava listened and drove as Hank called Jax. "So, you're available around seven at your house? Text me the address." Hank closed the call.

Ava glanced Hank's way. "You were the only appointment I had today. I need to be somewhere I feel safe. Will you stay with me until we see Jax?"

Hank looked at his watch. "It's almost lunchtime. We can pick something up and take it to your place."

As Ava drove into the garage, circling up and up to her parking spot, Hank chuckled. "What side of the building are you on?"

"Facing the canal." Ava bit her bottom lip. "I feel guilty because I've been watching for your lights at night."

They left the parked car and headed to the elevator. His worried expression melted into a grin. "You've been watching for me? If I'd known where you live, I'd have been watching for you."

As they rode in the elevator, Ava winked. "I'll bet you've got far better binoculars than I do."

Hank was impressed. "You have binoculars?"

****

Ava watched him take in her thoroughly feminine décor. All of the island-style furnishings were pastels and blonde wood. The largest things in the room were massive baskets holding birds of paradise and monstera plants in every corner. The inviting sofa was textured, ivory cotton long enough for a great nap.

She turned as she opened her bedroom door. "Hank, you were right. I'll feel better after a cool shower. Would you keep the food warm out there? I won't be long."

She heard soft jazz from the living room as she considered burning the outfit she wore; *it will only remind me of this morning. Good, he's not shy about making himself at home.*

In the shower, she tried to scrub away the dread of an unknown entity like the Triad. *They are the stuff of terrifying action movies.* Now they were her reality.

After using every bottle in her shower, Ava dried off with a bit less tension. But she had absolutely no appetite. With her bobbed hair nearly dry, she wrapped herself in her sateen robe and closed her eyes in thought for just a second. *How would he feel about me if I invited him back to hold me? … In my bed?*

When she opened her bedroom door, she peeked around the corner and saw Hank on the lanai. "Hank, will you come back here, please?"

His warm gaze covered her with appreciation and his words were slow and sweet like honey. "I'm all yours, Sunshine." Once they were toe to toe, Ava released the belt on her robe. Hank caught the fabric and held it together, maintaining his gaze into her eyes. "And I mean all yours." She saw the same golden sparkle she noticed on the plane.

"Will you hold me?" Her blood sang as he nodded. She unbuttoned his polo shirt as they stepped back to her king-size bed. Side by side they sat, both grinning at the bridge they were about to cross. Ava confessed. "I, ah… have a scar. Actually, a couple of them…"

Hank's fingers trailed across her hand and rested on her forearm. "But you're okay now, right?" He ran the backs of his fingers lightly over her cheek to brush her hair behind her ear.

"Oh, yeah, it's been years… a lumpectomy." Her hand cupped her right breast over her robe.

Hank's face grew concerned. "I wouldn't expect something like that to slow you down."

"You think?" Ava shrugged with a soft smile, and then her finger drew a line low across her belly. "And I'm a sports model since my hysterectomy."

Hank nodded as she blushed. "Sports model? I've never heard it described quite like that."

"Yeah, I'm one of those curated cars that never gets driven." Ava shrugged.

Hank smirked. "I cannot imagine why, you're a peach." He cocked his head comically. "I've got a scar. They cut me and I didn't walk for nine months."

Ava blanched and covered her mouth. "Oh, a war wound?"

Hank stood up. "I'd show you, but I'm seriously overdressed."

"Let me help you take care of that." Ava reached in offer to help, but Hank turned away briefly as he unbuckled his belt, let his trousers hit the floor and peeled down his boxer briefs.

"Ah, well…" He stood a bit sheepishly. Ava pulled back the quilt and watched to admire his backside. "See, the cut was my circumcision." He turned with his hands over his groin. "And I really didn't walk until I was almost ten months old."

Ava's smirk developed as she covered her mouth. "I'm not laughing at you… but I've never heard of it referred to in that way…" She reached for his hands. "Is it too late to kiss it and make it better?"

Hank chuckled softly as he joined her on the bedside. "You just need to cuddle, right? Otherwise, I came seriously unprepared."

She slid out of the robe, into the middle of the bed and held up the covers. Hank rolled to his side and stretched out. Dropping the covers over him, she laid a soft, slow kiss on his lips. She mumbled, "Right, just cuddle." Their lips parted as they exchanged breaths. "But if I just needed cuddling, we could have stayed dressed out on the sofa." Her flat hand skated across his chest and headed south, exploring his body, and working him into a heightened state of arousal. "Maybe I need something like holding each other and staring into each other's eyes so I know I have someone on my side."

"So, it isn't just about the lava flow?" Hank's grin spread as he wrapped his arms around her. "I'm a man who's given orders for decades. I bet you wonder how well I take direction?" His hand traveled the hill and slope of her contours.

"Oh, that sounds so sensitive." Ava stroked his jawline and pressed her fingertip to his lips. He caught her hand and kissed the palm, only to catch her finger with his lips. With a sly slip of his tongue, he suckled her fingertip. "Umm." She moaned as she arched against him. Ava drew in a deep breath as she climbed over his thighs. "Got any battle scars to show me?"

He looked wistful. "Nope…"

Her damp fingertip circled his shaft. "Aww, I can kiss this and make it better." Her intentions were teasing, but she recognized her hand had skated to circle his circumcised length and his response was positively impressive. "Isn't it amazing how empowering it is when you're with someone who makes you feel special?"

Hank caught her and rolled over her. "I'm feeling empowered, except for a condom." His reach extended to her thighs as his hands dove to cup her buttocks.

Their gazes locked warmly. "I can feel that. Now that we're here… I'm sure I'm good. How about you?" She waited with her eyes half-closed and a kittenish grin.

His body smoothly covered hers. "I'm good if you're good." He rested on his forearms and kissed her collarbone. "Don't you think from the minute I winked at you, we had something going? I'm free. You're free. This was going to happen, eventually." Hank's welcome weight felt like heaven. He cradled the breast with the well-healed scar and kissed it. "If it happened six months from now, we'd look back and see all the time we lost."

****

Aroused by the thought of Ava on the cool, clean sheets under him, his mind spun, imagining where he'd begin. Splayed on ivory bedding, her suntanned body displayed such an incredible contrast. Between her cologne and the sun's warmth, her complex cachet aroused him. "Sunshine, I'm going to devour you and when I'm done, you're going to taste yourself on my lips."

Hank buried his face in her sweet mound. Sucking her clit between his lips, he followed her sighs and moans as he worried the little bud of flesh with his tongue. His reward? She responded as a rosebud responds to sunlight. Her flesh enlivened, Ava spread her legs farther apart and shifted in invitation.

Hank came up to his knees. *This is going to happen.* That thought just about blew his mind. He shook his head at Ava. "If you hadn't invited me back here, we wouldn't be close like this." Although he throbbed for her wet heat, he anxiously returned between her legs. Looking up at her, he promised, "This is the way we should spend our nights."

He couldn't process rational thought as Ava tangled her fingers in his hair. She made lively mewling sounds while he savored tongue-fucking her. All Hank wanted at the moment was to turn off his logical brain and take her with delight to the heights of their pleasure. It was all coming back to him now, and it was amazing.

Hank had to admit he'd been freed by their fairy-tale meeting. Having never seen her in the preceding months while they corresponded by email, what were the chances? Hank got lost in discovering her pleasure points. In the back of his mind, he wondered if he met his love match on an airplane? *Talk about friendly skies.*

Some aspect of lightning struck judging by the long, low, guttural moan Ava released. Her knees gripped him in place. "Oh, Hank, please… more… ahhhhh."

With a chuckle, he lovingly pressed into her. She let go an angelic cry, some prayer to the heaven he built for her. Hank softened his attack and slowly brought her back to Earth. When he raised his head, Ava gulped for air. The blush glowed from under the sheen of her orgasmic response. "Feeling better now? Where's that tension?"

Ava rose on her elbows and covered her face with one hand. "My windows are open." Her knees came up, and she buried her face in her hands. "I opened the window to freshen up the room and my neighbors have heard everything.

On his knees, Hank stretched and grinned while her fingers caressed his treasure trail. "They should be happy for you. It may sound frivolous, but what we just did is the easiest way to get away from it all." He crawled up to her and pulled her into an embrace. "See, this is where I convince you to ride me… in a while."

Their bodies, slippery with lusty sweat, danced horizontally. They wrestled with the evil sheets intent on separating them. Hank pulled the top sheet aside and flung it to the end of the bed. "I always want to be this close to you." Hank stretched out in the center of the bed. After quite a few songs from the living room, Hank nuzzled Ava. "Have you ever ridden a rocket?"

****

Wide-eyed, Ava clutched her breasts. "A rocket? Oh, my stars."

The heat in his eyes scalded her as he lay back on the pillow, his arms behind his head. He winked at her. "I like the way you look in bed. I think I'll keep you here."

"Don't break my heart, Hank." Ava meant it. She'd risen from so many pyres in the past few years that her name should be Phoenix. At her age, where would she find a man like Hank?"

"I break the speed of sound, I break through enemy lines, but I'd never intentionally break your heart. This thing we're sharing. Does it leave you hungry for more?"

Ava's gaze randomly traveled over Hank's battle-fit body as she nodded yes. After their extended cuddling, interspersed with kisses, his stout erection revived. In his pride at his response to her eagerness, he gestured, "See what you do to me, just thinking about touching you. I'm hard, and this time I'm claiming every inch of your warm body."

"I see." Ava's tone took on a bit of smug self-satisfaction. She'd spent almost a year thinking he was a my-way-or-the-highway' kind of guy. Now she longed to see where that highway was headed.

****

Hank's hands urged her to straddle him, sitting forward. He enjoyed the sway of her breasts. Swept up in the novelty of his new cowgirl, Hank bit his bottom lip as her head fell back and she caught her breasts in her hands. *I this an invitation to fondle her as she rides me.*

With gusto, his hands caressed the slopes and the heavenly weight of her breasts. His breathing hitched as they fell into a driving rhythm. Words hissed out between his lips. "Ahhh, Sunshine, that, right there… just do that over and over…" Her head bobbed along with their strokes. Through the slits of his eyelids, he caught her saucy grin as his fists caught up the sheets.

****

Then, as if by some silent symbiosis, she picked up the cadence. Within her heart, she felt treasured and renewed by his unselfish sharing while skin to skin in her bed. Ava recognized the rhapsodic sounds of a man ridden to the hilt. She ground her hips on him and ran her fingertips along the side of his thighs. "You with me, handsome?"

He panted on the blessed edge of release. His moan was wordless and urgent. She leaned forward, glancing her breasts over his pecs. Two steely hands caught her hips as he begged, "Don't stop…"

Their 'connection' went on and on. Every cell in her body thrummed with anticipation. Passion's sweat spread across them; their bodies flushed. When his heart thrummed double-time, she felt his burning grasp as he drew her down to him.

With lusty energy, Hank sat up and pulled her onto his lap. In the middle of the bed, he sat, legs crossed and his arms around her.

"Ooh, I always wanted to try this…" Ava cooed as she wrapped her legs behind his back and molded into his embrace.

Hilt deep within her, their hips moved in harmony as Hank thrust lovingly. Their bodies fused on so many levels. He was beautiful to her, his face flushed with arousal. With his loving attentions, she felt beautiful. More importantly, she felt treasured. As her heart measured how long they could stay just like this, his warm eyes clenched shut and his mouth fell away from her kisses. She felt his body roar into hers and collapsed with him. They shook together and fell to the bed, beyond satisfied.

Holding their warmth under the covers, Ava spooned to his front. She spun in his arms to look him in the face. "I thought you said it's been a while?"

Hank traced her moving lips with his fingertip. "Out in that RV, all I had were memories and my imagination."

Saucily, Ava retorted. "Well, I suppose we could explore our imaginations to enjoy this a lot." Hank nodded. Grinning, he ran a hand over his upper lip and sighed. She shyly asked. "Unless you need to be somewhere, let's just be here."

****

Hank followed the smell of over-warmed food. With a chuckle, he looked at the time. *Who kept who busy for the last five hours?* He stretched his back and rotated his shoulders. *These are the slow workouts I can get behind.* "Hey, Sunshine, our lunch is toast."

Ava glided down the hall on a cloud. "Toast? Lunch? We can pick up ramen on the way to Jax's. You did work up my hunger." She approached him from behind and threw her arms around his waist. Resting her cheek on his back, she sighed. "You have such a strong heartbeat."

Hank turned within her embrace to take her face in his hands. "Well, now you know, aerobic activity is good for a geezer like me."

She chuckled slyly. "Geezer, right…"

****

Ava and Hank arrived right behind Kirk and Jordan at the House of Double Happiness. "I just love houses with names. It's like an estate."

"Don't kid yourself. It is an estate. You should see the security system." Hank waved to his friend. "Hey, Romeo, who's that good-looking babe you have with you?"

Kirk snickered. "I could ask you the same."

Hank turned to a blushing Ava. "Sunshine, you remember Jordan and Kirk Roman."

Ava extended her hand. "I love when my events begin long marriages."

Jordan came in for a hug. "Nothing like a backyard wedding when the backyard is on the ocean."

As Kirk shook Hank's hand, one brow rose. He whispered, "Hey, Teflon, you and your lady using the same body wash?"

Hank straightened his shirttail. "None of your damn business."

Kameo threw open the front door. "Is the party out here?"

"Why not?" Ava held her arms out expansively. "What an exquisite estate."

Doobie pattered up, yawned, and threw himself down at Kameo's feet. "Just walk around the big, frightening pit bull mix. Great watchdog, huh?"

"Ooh, a watchdog. Perhaps I should get one of those?" Ava asked.

****

After Jax exhausted every question, his wife, Kameo, and Jordan went to the kitchen to set up dinner on the lanai.

Hank got back to business. "I'm worried about Ava." He placed his hand over hers and they exchanged a glance. "She has no close relatives, and she lives alone." With a nod, he moved his hand off hers.

Ava shrugged. "I'm such a workaholic I have employees, acquaintances, and business associates. What else is there for me than work?"

All three men raised their brows at her and Jax answered, "If you have to ask that question, you're not living right."

Hank glowered at Jax. "Oh, like you weren't totally dedicated to your team for years. It took mustering out for you to slow down."

Jax caught Kameo's hand. "Baby, have I slowed down?"

Kameo looked at him from under her lashes, and then she grinned at the people at the table. "Next month, he's going to be the third frogman in an action movie filmed on the North Shore."

Hank's jaw went slack. "'Third frogman,' huh?"

Jax waved him off. "I'm also the dive coordinator. It's a long story."

****

They continued to pick at pineapple and mangos as they discussed Ava's predicament. Kirk frowned. "What's the name of the other tenant in your building?"

"Huang." Ava shrugged. "His last name is Huang. Apparently, there are several Huangs involved."

Jax consulted his tablet. "Xiang Huang? She shook her head. "Dai Huang?" She shook again. Jax smirked at this one. "His father had to have some twisted sense of humor to name his son "Peng Huang." Jax's belly laugh fell like a lead zeppelin. "What?"

Ava looked hard at Hank and reached for his hand. "That's him, Peng Huang."

Kirk laughed. "Might as well be a boy named Sue."

Ava looked grim. "The name may be funny, but the man is not."

The men around the table sobered. Ava asked the obvious question. "So, what can I do?"

Jax rubbed at the crease between his brows. "First thing in the morning, I'm going to get on the phone with my contacts on the mainland. Let's find out if Peng Huang is in the system."

Kirk drummed a beat on the table. "I'll contact Evan Silver. See what he can dig up on the various Huangs. And Hank, we'll visit my security guy." Kirk nodded to Ava. "You'll be airtight once they fix you up."

****

It was a culture shock. Hank retired to get out of airstrikes and overseeing military actions. He was home to celebrate his daughter's wedding and the good woman who had done so much to make their plans a beautiful reality was being terrorized. On top of that, he had a growing spot in his heart for Ava. It wasn't the call of a damsel in distress. Her personality revved his engines. And from the satisfied look on her face, she didn't notice he forgot about all that 'tantric' control. They'd loved each other with an honestly natural hunger.

After they had made their good nights at Jax and Kameo's, Hank drove them back to Ava's condo. "We'll stop at your place so you can pack a few things." Ava's eyes went wide. "I've got a three-bedroom condo, pick a room, any room, but stay with me."

"Hank, we had a wonderful afternoon, but you don't owe me that. My condo is safe."

Hank didn't argue. "Look, let me walk you to your door. I'll do a walkthrough and then you can lock up behind me. I'll walk home."

Feeling good about their decision, they rode the elevator with smiles on their faces. Ava looked up at Hank. "Your family is extraordinary; your folks really understand Ohana."

The elevator door opened and within a few steps, Ava saw her front door ajar. Hank held up a cautioning hand. "Pull out your phone. I'll go in."

"Like hell!" She pulled out her phone.

Hank turned on his heel and led her to the chair in the elevator lobby. "I want us where we can see anyone who might leave your apartment." As Ava called 911, she cocked her head for Hank to follow her. She opened the stairwell door with the small window, and they stood by the trash chute watching the hall and elevator in vain.

*** * * ***

The young patrol cop walked the apartment first and confirmed it was empty. After an almost pointless meeting, the officer made a report and left. Ava packed an overnight bag while Hank righted chairs and closed drawers.

She drummed her fingers on her steering wheel as they headed to Hank's condo. Ava gritted her teeth. "It serves me right. I installed a security system, and I never set the alarm. They jimmied the lock, got in, tore the place up, and walked out with nothing I could see. Don't you love how the officer wagged his finger at me?"

Hank sat restlessly in the passenger seat. "Yeah, and he didn't seem to agree it's related to your warehouse theft. That's ignorant."

*** * * ***

At Hank's place, ever the gracious host, he opened the hall closet and pulled out fresh towels. Standing in the hallway, he nodded to

Ava. "You have your choice. Will it be the yellow, white, or beige bathroom?"

Ava stood, biting her bottom lip. "Which one is yours?"

Hank's grin widened. "Follow me and find out." He flipped on two sets of lights in the master bath. "The shower is that way. Sky must have expected guests. See how she made that basket with a new toothbrush and lady stuff?"

"Lady stuff?" Ava slid beside Hank and regarded them in the long wall mirror. She looked up at him saucily. "Oh, *Sky* did this, huh?"

Hank tapped the swan faucet on the Jacuzzi tub. "This baby has heaters, and it bubbles."

Ava's gaze traveled from the graceful tub fixtures to Hank. "Who designed this bathroom?"

Hank chuckled as he hung Ava's towels on the empty rack. "You can thank Jordan; I bought the place from her."

They turned and Ava almost doubled over in laughter. Hank asked dryly, "What?"

Ava gestured to the huge TV opposite the bed. One nightstand held a stack of Michael Connolly books, the TV remote, and a small pitcher and cup. "I guess I know which side is yours."

Hank walked across the room and drew the drapes. "Hey, there's a nightstand on your side for whatever you want…"

Carrying her overnight bag to the chair on her side, she looked over her shoulder and smiled. "Why don't we meet in the middle?"

Hank winked and threw up his index finger. "Let me go brush my teeth. Then we can concentrate on that life/work balance issue."

****

The following morning, Hank woke up with the most remarkable feeling. His bed was warm, the sheets smelled like them,

67

and when he opened his eyes, she gazed at him with a sly smile. "Did you stare me awake?"

"Maybe." She rolled on her side and punched up the pillow. "I haven't slept in a warm bed since I can't remember."

Hank rolled on his side and smirked. "Are you a vampire? Do you sleep in a freezer?" He ran his hand over his scruffy neck.

She reached for that hand and threaded her fingers in his. "No, silly. It's just you are such a teddy bear. This bed sizzles."

Hank drew her closer and kissed her on the forehead. "It's all you, Sunshine. You brought the magic."

"We have two choices…"

"Two choices?" His voice wavered. "Okay, you pick."

****

Ava picked the first choice, and they didn't make it to the kitchen for another hour. As she puttered around with coffee, she shook her head. "When is that new stove arriving?"

"Apparently, it takes a while when you live in Hawaii. Sky brought me a toaster oven."

Ava looked nervously at the clock. "I regret having to go back into that building, but I need to get into my office."

Hank opened the freezer door. "Waffles, breakfast bowls, sausage biscuits, take your pick." He ran his hand over his scruff. "What's the dress code on beards?"

"What does that have to do with breakfast bowls?" She held up her hand as she scrutinized the full freezer.

"Not a damn thing, but let me shave my face and I'll be your bodyguard. Any dress code I should be aware of?"

Ava set the toaster oven for the breakfast bowls and shooed him out of the kitchen. "I'll order you one of our Aloha shirts. Get cracking. I'm a hard taskmaster."

Before Hank shut the bathroom door, he quipped, "I know."

Chapter Six

Hank drove Ava to work and took his bodyguard job seriously, insisting on walking the office before he let her in. Opening the door, he got this morning's shock. "Wow, Mano, they really got you bad."

Mano spun on his task chair with bruises blossoming dark blue and purple. "Yeah, they did. Good morning, Ms. Hansen." Ava slowly approached the man she had come to rely on as her right hand. He looked worse than he did yesterday. "Did something else happen?"

Mano hung his head for a beat. "Ms. Hansen, they paid a visit to my house. Luckily, no one was home. But I can't have this. I have kids."

Ava's shoulders slumped. "I understand." Her words came out in a whisper. She turned to Hank. "Would you have any place for a trustworthy manager?"

Hank scratched the back of his neck. "Well, I will in about a month. I'm thinking Silver Seal might be able to use a good man." He looked at Mano. "I believe this is a temporary snafu, Mano. You and Ava will be working together again soon."

As Mano nodded, a smile returned to his face. "That would give me great peace of mind."

Ava patted his shoulder. "Hank is going to be my bodyguard; you go home and rest. I'll be in touch."

As soon as Ava saw Mano's car move down the road, her phone rang, and she put it on speaker. Before she could answer, the voice struck a nerve. "Ms. Hansen, this is Peng Huang. You left a message on my answering machine."

"Yes…"

"Regarding the supposed mix-up in deliveries. I'm afraid you're mistaken. Our warehouse never received any delivery for you, and the delivery truck admits we did not sign for the skid of shoes." There was a pregnant pause before he continued. "Someone at your address did. I need my shoes or one hundred and seventy-eight thousand dollars."

"Mr. Huang, you know very well my warehouse was broken into and cleaned out."

The voice on the phone was cool. "I did hear something about your loss. That, however, is your problem. I still need either my shoes or the money."

Hank paced the floor, glaring in Huang's general direction. When Ava's mouth opened to speak, Hank put a finger on her lips. "Mr. Huang, our legal department is working on that. We'll be in touch." Hank smirked as he ended the call.

Ava squealed, "Legal department. Are you delusional?" Her gaze darted from bookcase to bookcase and her computers. "I've got to get out of here. I hope to God they don't tail me, but I've got to get what's left out of here."

Hank nodded. "Let me make a call." He dialed Kirk and Jordan answered. "Hey, had a bit of a morning today. I need two guys who don't mind mixing it up to help me pack up Ava's office. You know anybody like that?"

Jordan's voice was hesitant. "Is Ava okay?"

Ava spoke up. "I'm good. I just need to move a few things into a safe place."

****

Ava, being the last person out of the office, locked up for whatever good that did and taped a sign on the front door. "Closed due to water damage."

Kirk looked over his shoulder as Jax drove the truck away. "I've been thinking, there's a tax preparer's office next door to our gym.

This is their off-season and there's no one there. I bet they'd sublet to you for a few weeks."

Ava nodded enthusiastically. "Is that where you sent Jax?"

"Well, yeah, I sent him to our parking garage until you make a decision. We have security, and the parking lot is gated."

****

Jordan greeted Ava at the door with tea. "Ava, honey, I made you some chamomile tea. For today, I'm going to set you up in my back office. The password for the Wi-Fi is inside the desk drawer. Make yourself at home.

Ava hugged Jordan and clung on for an extra second. "I don't know where I'd be without you all. I've got a list of appointments to reschedule."

Jordan maintained her serenity. "You know this is the time you reach out to all those people who appreciate your attention to detail. Call them and tell them your office has water damage. You want to meet clients here."

Ava dropped her purse on the desk. "You're amazing." She took the tea and lowered herself into the chair, enjoying the fragrant steam. "Thanks for thinking of this. I'll take a moment and calm down."

"Don't you worry, in the past six years we've overcome some strange… shenanigans." Jordan left and closed the door behind her.

****

The men assembled in the secure pool house that doubled as the Roman armory. Jax spoke as he powered up the equipment in the room. "I asked my buddy Gideon to do an off-the-record investigation on Peng Huang. The police aren't doing squat. Something's going on and I want to know why."

"Damn straight." Hank moved to a chair and sat down. His gaze traveled over the room and its contents. "This is set up like a damn command center." The conference table held protected communications equipment. Three walls of diamond-plate held a formidable selection of weapons. Half of the short wall was an ammo safe.

Jax dialed Gideon Sullivan. When the video call engaged, Hank, who expected a hard-edged Fed, was surprised to see a tanned and golden-haired guy in a surfer's tank top. The secure line's monitor displayed Gideon with beach hair. "Do you guys know what time it is? I'm on vacation."

Jax shook his head. "Crime doesn't take vacations."

Gideon swiped through his wild hair. "And you don't expect me to, either." Gideon nodded to his camera. "I see a new face. Hi, I was Jax's wrangler on the DEA Taskforce."

Jax shook his head. "Gid, let me introduce Major General Hank Kingston, Air Force Retired. He and my dad go way back. Hank, Gideon is a US Marshal. I taught him everything he knows so he could replace me on the joint task force."

"You taught me? I taught you." Gideon folded muscular arms over his chest as he nodded to Jax. "Is that what this call is about?" Gideon squinted at the image of Jax's room on his computer monitor. "You still have that arsenal set up at your house? For crap's sake, Jax, I thought you were out of this business."

Hank spoke up. "You can take the man out of the action… I'm afraid I've roped him into a situation."

Jax gestured smugly. "Has all this not been useful?"

Kirk nodded to Gideon, "He's got you there."

Hank folded his arms over his chest and harrumphed. "What about this human stain that put Ava out of business?"

Jax sat and turned to the computer camera. "I don't understand this, Gid. It's as if the HPD is afraid of this guy. I mean, one shipment of hers went next door and when her employee inquired about it, he got busted up. Ava's guy is a native, and he said they look like Triad;

they beat the hell out of him. That night, her warehouse was cleaned out. Her home and her assistant's home were vandalized. And she was threatened on the phone this morning. The police act like it was all her fault."

Gideon leaned his chin on his palm as he listened. "Triad?" He sucked air through his teeth. "What is this guy's name?"

Jax nodded. "Peng Huang. Why is HPD so shy?"

Gideon typed into his computer and then grunted over several thousand miles. "I'll tell you why. This super slime is the son of the People's Republic of China's Ambassador to the United States."

Hank thumped the table. "Balls."

Gideon agreed. "You are not wrong, and this is not the first time Peng Huang has had a tantrum."

Hank and Kirk shared an incredulous look. "Seriously, his name is Peng Huang?"

"Yeah, around our office they call him Pen-guin, and the worse part? He has a thing for tuxedos. It's laughable. Anyway, last Chinese New Year he had a party that burned down a wing of a hotel in San Francisco. That little stunt just about got his family recalled to China. They shuffled him out to Hawaii."

Hank growled. "So, the entitled little bastard has diplomatic immunity." Jax nodded. "Anyone else would be in jail by now. But he's protected."

Gideon continued. "There have been rumors that Ambassador Huang and his sainted firstborn are running drugs, gambling, and women on your little island home."

"Human trafficking?" Hank leaned into the conversation.

Gideon grimaced. "Let's call it was it is, slavery in the sex trade."

Hank shook his head. "How can the authorities just ignore this?"

Gideon shrugged. "The HPD will turn a blind eye unless you can prove the illegal activities of the whole gang and arrest his foot soldiers."

Jax sighed. "Well, that would be a good trick. I suppose the DEA can't help either."

Gideon held up his hands in surrender. "No representative of the United States government can do a goddamn thing." The men grumbled. "On the other hand, concerned citizens who happen to have certain skills may feel inclined to corral this threat to their community. Maybe they could get the whole Huang family recalled to China and their activities shut down."

Jax laughed. "We'll need the usual toys…"

Gideon smirked as he pointed at the weapons on the wall. "Toys? I thought you had them all."

****

Hank left the 'pool house on steroids' and surveilled the lavish patio. From there to Diamondhead Road, exquisitely manicured mini estates were lined tightly. He turned to Jax. "Nice quarters. Do you know your neighbors?" The home next door featured a larger pool area and permanent fitness equipment.

With a hearty chuckle, Jax elbowed Hank. "The gal next door is a pro surfer turned film star and works out with her trainer boyfriend. When we're worn out, Kameo and I make popcorn and watch them like TV."

"It's so quiet here, I can hear the surf." Hank turned to take in the height of the walls, the motion sensor lights, and the other security features. "You have yourself a fortress."

Jax surveilled his surroundings and grinned. "Yes, I do."

CHAPTER SEVEN

The following morning, Jordan let out a giggle as she knocked on Hank's door. It was nothing in particular, and it was everything. Here in the midst of panic and pandemonium, her old friend Hank, who she always called 'Kingy' had a houseguest. From Kirk's ramblings before he fell asleep last night, evidently Kingy was sharing body wash with 'Sunshine.'

She righted her face as she heard Ava answering the door with a cautious, "Who is it?" in a phony, deepened voice.

"It's Jordan." She smiled as Ava opened the door. "I go to the market in samurai shopping mode. It always lifts my spirits. Won't you come with me?"

Ava grinned. "Yes! You know this house has too much man food. Nothing fun for me to zap in the microwave."

As they drove away, Jordan noticed Ava's smile returning. "I can't wait for some retail therapy. Sometimes, it's great to be in the store, finding everything you have your heart set on."

Ava rested back and basked in the breeze. "As well as a few serendipitous discoveries."

The ladies pushed two carts through the market until Jordan's basket was tapped by another. Jordan stopped mid-sentence to Ava and swiveled back to see the careless driver. Words died on her lips. *That son of a bitch.*

Not even looking up, the man mumbled, "Sorry." Or something that passed as an apology. Part of her wanted to ram back just to see if he'd raise his head. Part of her wanted to shift in reverse and avoid Wade Stieber altogether. Ava shot her a look as Jordan stood planted in his path; a frozen expression of disgust painted on her heretofore happy face.

"Hello, Wade." She drew out his name like a curse word and watched Ava blink.

The man finally looked up from the wine labels he studied. "Jordie, honey, where have you been? Long time no see. I missed you at the boat show. I see you have a friend!"

Jordan stood protectively in front of Ava and did not introduce her. "Well, I am not hard to find. I am at the gym five days a week. You remember Silver Seal, don't you?"

Wade's expression drained as his palm rested on his flat abdomen. "I couldn't forget it for the world. How is Mr. Super-SEAL? I think I've got a job for him." He pushed his cart to the side and motioned them to follow him. "That beast of a SEAL, he must have a certain set of skills that he isn't currently monetizing."

Jordan cocked her head. "Excuse me?"

"What I'm saying is this job would pay handsomely." He rubbed his fingers and thumb together, indicating money. "Are you still working there?"

She dropped her chin, and her mouth became a straight line. "Yes." Jordan leaned back from the conversation and slid her left hand into her pocket. "Why do you ask?"

"Well, the skills he gained over a career like his come in high demand these days."

"Do they? Once again, what do I have to do with it?"

Wade took an anonymous-looking business card out of his wallet. He jotted his name on the back along with the note, 'job offer'. When he handed it to Jordan, she slowly examined both sides. "Why would you need a SEAL, aren't you a Ranger?"

Wade stood a little taller and folded his arms over his chest. "I'll be coordinating the mission; I can't be in two places at once. A team leader needs the best."

Still, regarding the odd card, Jordan didn't look up. "He'll be happy to know the buzz is good." She looked up to see Wade posing in the wine aisle, his smile flashing at the beach babe behind her. Jordan held up the card. "I'll pass it on. I'm sure if he's interested, he'll call." She couldn't move away fast enough.

Once they were in the next aisle, Ava made a face. "I didn't know slime could walk. Did you see him checking out the bunny behind you?"

Jordan narrowed her eyes. "It walks *and* talks." They took a few steps. "I don't know when I learned to lie like that!"

Ava smirked back and shrugged. "I'm sure there's a long story there somewhere."

Jordan shook her head. "Not so long. Kirk saved me from what could have been a bad situation with that guy. Saying he's a predator would not be too strong a word." Jordan looked at the kimchi on the shelf to her left. "He will not ruin my day." The thought of seeing Wade Stieber evaporated from her mind the moment they loaded groceries into the car.

****

That evening Kirk Roman padded around, locking doors, and turning out lights. It was the first quiet night in a long time. "I'm taking wine into the Jacuzzi. Want to join me?"

"Well, sure." Jordan followed him and held out her arms. "I love when you undress me."

Kirk lowered the lights and Jordan lit candles. His crooked grin widened. "I do enjoy that part of life." He began lowering her skort when a business card fell to the floor. "You've got a business card here." He looked at it closely. "This is weird, just a phone number?" He turned over the card. "Wade Stieber?" He shook the card. "Job offer?" His expression turned offended. "You wouldn't…"

"No, I wouldn't. He was looking for you, Mr. SEAL. He said he had a mission for you." She made air quotes at the word. "I forgot to tell you; he ran into me at the market."

Kirk shook the card. "I hate this guy. What the hell does he want with me?"

Jordan shrugged. "He said, and I quote, 'it pays handsomely.' And to hear him tell it, he will 'coordinate the mission.'"

Kirk snorted. "He couldn't coordinate a flag ceremony."

Jordan laughed. "Well, if you can stomach him, he wants *you*." She pointed at him like Uncle Sam.

Kirk waved the card. "I'm going to get to the bottom of this just to see what he's up to. I don't trust that smarmy bastard."

Jordan snatched the card from Kirk's fingertips. "Enough about him. Back to the fun."

****

The odd business card Jordan gave him last night sat on the dresser. Kirk carried it to the kitchen when he left a satisfied and drowsy Jordan snuggling into his pillow. How else do you leave your wife when your past competition accidentally bumps into her at the market? *The asshole has probably been stalking her. Job offer? What is going on in that man's convoluted mind?*

Sleepy-eyed, Jordan tiptoed up behind Kirk and grabbed him around the waist. "Good morning. Quit looking at the card and just call the jerk."

Kirk grinned. "Let's see if he's an early riser." It was five-fifty-five. The phone answered on the second ring. "Stieber." The voice was thick with last night's drink.

"Stieber, I heard you were looking for an able-bodied crew."

"Roman?" The name rolled thickly off the other man's tongue.

"You essentially called me. What's this mission you're coordinating?" Kirk heard the rustle of sheets and Wade's morning groans.

"I need surveillance on a competitor."

"You need surveillance on a competing boat blogger?"

Stieber coughed up half a lung. *I knew he was a smoker.* "Hell no, not a blogger. This is another target. I have an associate, Mr. Huang, in the business of Chinese imports." Kirk was immediately on alert. "It's his competitor. The guy's in Honolulu on vacation. If we can catch him in some compromising photos, they might force him to come to an agreement."

Kirk's spine stiffened as he ground his teeth, biting back his anger to sound nonchalant. "Let me think about this. I don't know if I want to go all PI for you, Wade."

Wade hacked as Kirk heard him light a cigarette. "If I wanted a PI, I wouldn't have called you."

"I'll call you back in an hour or two. Maybe we can work something out." Kirk's face bloomed in anger when he sat his cell down.

Jordan gave him a skeptical look. "Maybe we can work something out?"

Kirk's eyes blazed. "That son of a bitch. It's been days since the HPD has said anything about Ava's problems. We've heard nothing. And we know why. Peng's father is the Chinese ambassador, and that little punk has diplomatic immunity." Kirk moved around the kitchen stormily, slamming his mug down to pour his coffee, and viciously unpeeling a banana. He pointed the fruit at Jordan. "When Stieber said his associate was Huang in Chinese imports, I thought, 'yeah, you think that's a coincidence?'" Jordan leaned back from him. "And yeah, it's the same damn name. I'm calling Jax and his DEA buddy. I'm going to put a fire under your old flame."

Jordan shuddered. "He's no flame of mine."

Kirk checked himself. His appeasing grin gave way to a chuckle. "He thought sending you a potted arrangement of baboon dicks was a smooth move."

"Those were anthuriums, Kirk, an expensive tropical plant."

"Which oddly is still thriving outside our gym regardless of the number of cigarettes people stub out in the pot."

Jordan strolled into her husband's embrace. "But you're the one who won my heart."

He kissed the tip of her nose. "You're my anchor, Jordie." He held her in a renewing embrace.

****

Kirk tapped the Bluetooth and dialed his son. When Jax answered, Kirk hit his blinker and dodged into the morning rush of traffic. "What are the odds one of Huang's footmen wants to hire me to surveil his competition?"

Kirk heard Jax's astonishment. "Zip. When did this happen?"

Kirk kept an eye on the rear-view mirror. "Jordan was approached yesterday. I have a business card your DEA friend should see. How fast can we conference at the gym?

"I'll call Hank and see you in fifteen minutes."

****

Jax trotted down the gym's stairs to join Kirk in his office. Within minutes, Hank joined them. "We have a mission." Jax grabbed up bottled water and tossed it to Hank.

"Oh, yeah?" Hank opened the bottle, downed a swig, and swallowed; his attention drawn through the glass window into the gym. Those weren't spandex-covered gym rats, but a group of women Jordan and Ava's age grooving to the music.

Jax cleared his throat and Hank snapped to attention. "We have a lead on Huang."

Hank's interest accelerated. "About time." Hank patted his pockets for his phone and his keys. "I can't wait to get my hands on that bastard."

Jax placed a flat hand in the center of Hank's chest. "But there's more…"

Kirk's fingers flew over the computer keyboard, accessing old members. "This guy, Wade Stieber, has hooked up with Huang somehow."

Hank wandered to peer over Kirk's shoulder, alive with interest. "Explain."

"He's not on the level. I don't even trust what he says about his service record. But he does seem to know Huang and that could be an in for us."

Hank gestured Kirk out of his seat. "I might still have some credentials. Let's see what I dig up." An honest picture of Wade Stieber's service record emerged as Kirk paced impatiently.

Jax watched images appear, he shook his head and dialed Gideon. "Gid, I've got Kirk and Hank on speaker behind closed doors. We need your help."

Gideon's tone of voice reflected he'd read Jax's email. "Yeah, I think you do. Tell me about this guy, Stieber."

Jax read the official report. "Born in Wisconsin, joined the Army at seventeen when a juvenile court gave him the choice of enlisting or incarceration. Seemed to straighten out under Army discipline. Rose to the rank of Corporal…"

Hank interrupted indignantly. His restlessness was obvious with that bouncing knee. "That's a little different from what did he tell you, Romeo, a Looie in the Rangers?"

Jax looked up at his friend from under his lashes, his voice low and calming. He carried on as if there were no interruption. "He was a Unit Clerk in Iraq and then Kuwait."

Gideon piped up. "Where are you getting this, Jax?"

Jax chuckled. "You're not my sole resource. I've beaten tougher interrogators than you. Hold on, Hank's got something."

Hank's jaw clenched as his thumbs worked the keyboard. "Stieber… is a sneaky son of a bitch…guess we knew that! He was a clerk who always carried a pocket full of Viagra… had a still for rotgut vodka as well as a small grow farm for bad dope. Nothing terribly serious stateside, but in Kuwait, a grave violation of their laws. Sure enough, he ran a scam on the wrong person and the Kuwaitis got involved."

Jax leaned back on the edge of the desk with a confirming smirk. "That explains his Court Martial as an embarrassment to the United States Government. He was convicted on behavior unbecoming and given a dishonorable discharge."

Gideon's voice traveled the few thousand miles from San Diego. "So, he's still a delinquent. How's he wrapped up with Peng?"

Jax rolled a pen between his fingers. "He's making noises about hiring Kirk to work for his employer, 'Mr. Huang.' Supposedly, they need surveillance on a competitor."

Gideon grumbled, "Who's the competitor?"

Kirk ground his fist into his hand. "I don't know…yet…we're alerting you before I meet with him. If things go sideways, I'll need some support."

Gideon's chair groaned across the speaker. "The guy said his boss was Mr. Huang? You got the first name?"

Kirk ran a hand through his hair. "Don't know yet, but this damn poser said his boss is in Chinese Imports. I'd bet the farm it's the scum extorting Ava."

There was silence for a beat on Gideon's end.

Kirk leaned toward Jax's phone; his tone was intense. "You intimated some 'concerned citizens' could nail Peng and get the

Huang family recalled to China. We need solid information on the players to succeed. That's what we're asking for. Let me tell you, Gid, Wade Stieber is a damn fraud! He came in here years ago bragging about being a Ranger. He even wears Ranger ink!" The three military veterans' expressions darkened dangerously. "Years ago, this swinging dick didn't know I had my eye on Jordan. While I was putting him through a gym workout, he laid out a scam to me about getting Jordan alone on a boat in the middle of the ocean, where she couldn't get away from him. I put a kink in that plan, and I wouldn't put anything past him."

Hank's lip curled. "And now he's tied up with this Huang bastard! What can you get for us, Gideon?"

Gideon was decisive. "Kirk, accept that job and find out who the competitor is. Meanwhile, I'll look at Peng Huang's associates. If this Stieber guy has something to do with the head of the snake, it should be relatively easy to find out. You call me back when you have your info." Kirk and Hank stood, all but ready to take the man on with their bare hands. "Listen," Gideon's voice was grave. "Listen to me. A job offer may not be all Stieber is after. If he is connected, they may have been following you, somehow associating you with Ava. Watch your six at this meeting." He clicked off the call.

Jax rocked off the end of the desk and motioned the two men closer. "Dad, Gid's right. There's too much hothead coming off you two. I understand it. The son of a bitch went after your women, but you've both planned enough missions to know you've got to make the plan and stay cool. All this heat will get you burned."

Kirk stared unseeing out the office window. Hank studied his hands. After a beat, Kirk gusted a sigh and turned. "I know you're right, Jax. I know you're right."

"It's different when it could have been your lady," Hank murmured, unclenching his hands. "But I agree. We've gotta keep our heads in the game and forget the emotions."

Jax nodded solemnly. Kirk pulled Wade's business card out of his pocket and dialed.

"Mr. Stieber's phone," a silky voice answered.

"Yeah. Lemme talk to the Ranger."

"Will you hold for a moment, please?" There was a beat of silence. "Excuse me, who's calling?"

Kirk answered brusquely. "Kirk Roman."

The silky voice didn't mute the call. A harpy shriek emitted from Kirk's speaker, "WADE! Kirk Roman's on the phone for you." Silence. Then, "WADE, are you done in the bathroom? I gotta do my hair."

The three men sat in horrified bemusement. A weary voice came to the phone. "Stieber."

"This is Roman. About that job? When can we meet?"

"Is enrollment down at the gym?"

"We're fine, thanks. Just thought it might be fun to do a little spycraft. Do you want me or not?"

"Meet me at the last dock at The Sailing Club, off Sand Island access road. I'll be on the pier in front of The Vesper today at two. You won't miss me. It's the meanest-looking black boat in the harbor."

Kirk hung up his phone and rolled his eyes. "So much for the amateur hour! Geesh! Vesper? Seriously? Why is my life becoming a sixties spy rip-off?"

Chapter Eight

With Kirk gone, Ava, Jordan, and Kameo returned to work. Hank and Jax met at his armory and drew plastic and old blankets over the conference table. In preparation, they unpacked Jax's arsenal and cleaned guns while they posited the tasks ahead.

****

Peng Huang scrolled through the intel on the iPad with satisfaction. "This man is thorough?"

Wade Stieber stood before the Triad boss. "He thinks he can make mincemeat out of me. He is thorough."

****

Kirk flipped on his sunnies and drove off. Was he paranoid, or did he need a means of communication they couldn't trace? Leaving his phone locked in the trunk, Kirk picked up the gas station burner phone and pocketed it.

In the vicinity of the basin, Kirk snapped photos of every license plate. At the end of the last pier, he saw The Vesper, a hulking giant of an ebony superyacht. She rested two-hundred-nineteen feet at anchor, dwarfing every other vessel. The electronics alone were the size of a car. Kirk squinted into the sun. *Is that a helipad? I'll bet they use the hell out of that! It could come in handy.*

From under the trees at the restaurant, Kirk snapped multiple photos of the ship. Sadly, zooming in at ten-time strength, he still couldn't count how many were aboard. He messaged the photos to Jax and reset the burner back to factory settings.

He checked his watch. It was one-fifteen, so he slipped into the tiki bar for a club soda. Kitschy décor and twangy island music reminded him why he shied away from tourist traps. Kirk took a seat positioned to watch the pier and head down over his swizzle stick, he watched a departing group gather on deck. Some shook hands, some bowed, and ten people left the yacht. The men wore business suits, the women in chic, black sheaths carried expensive handbags. Kirk slid from his seat and headed toward the bathroom. He hid within the palm fronds to shoot photos of the people as they separated in three different directions to smaller speedboats. *Now those are some great identifying shots.* Once they were forwarded to Jax, he repeated resetting the phone and returned to his club soda. He studied the sleek lines of the flat-black hull. *Man, you must be 'this rich' to get on that yacht.*

Kirk left his barstool and leaned against a tall palm tree. A gaggle of toned and tanned women strolled past all the other yachts to stop while being granted permission to board The Vesper.

Ducking behind the palm, he caught a glance through his camera's ten times lens. Topless women in bikinis and pareos danced on the top deck. *Change of shift? Anyone else would be cited for public nudity.* The ladies from the gangway joined the ladies on the top deck. *There have to be at least twenty.*

At one-fifty-five, Kirk strolled up to Wade Stieber at the end of the dock. Wade looked at his gaudy watch. "You're early."

Kirk checked his Aquaracer. "It's 1:56. Being on time is late. Let's get this done."

Wade led him to the gangway and gestured him to the side deck. "Welcome aboard, Squid. You don't mind a security check, do you?" Two hulking bookends of muscle appeared from the saloon. Wade fairly delivered Kirk into their arms. Once inside the saloon, Kirk's hat and phone were inspected. He was asked to step out of his shoes and was intimately patted down.

Leaning over the mustard-gold-silk divan, Kirk chided, "Wade, after that pat-down, I feel like I really know you, or at least your brothers here."

No one cracked as much as a smirk. With the same silent movement, the bookends were gone and replaced with twin bikini-clad ladies. Wade directed Kirk to sit on the furniture he'd been bent over. Wade posed at the neo-classical bar with the ladies who began serving from an anonymous decanter. "Join me for a drink?"

Kirk sat rigidly. "I don't drink on the job."

The twins sighed sadly. Wade scoffed as he accepted his glass and a peck on the cheek from twin number one. "Your loss, the eighteen-year-old single malt Japanese whisky, is inimitable."

Twin number two sat at the other end of the divan with a pouty look. Kirk's mind spun. *Does Wade know the meaning of his words? Is this the same buffoon who tried to scam Jordan?* Kirk shrugged and waited. Wade accepted another two fingers of whisky and paced as he spoke. *Does this guy stay pickled all the time? That could be an advantage.*

"This is pretty simple stuff, Squid." He looked at the girls with a juvenile smile and shooed them away like you dispatch dogs. Once they sulked off, Wade continued, "This man," he tossed an enlarged photo to the table before Kirk. "Syaoran Tengfeng is nipping at my boss's heels. This disturbs my boss. My boss believes since he works with one foot in China and one foot in the United States, the import business should be as balanced. Mr. Tengfeng is an upstart who we believe has arrived to discredit the good name of the Huang family."

Kirk smirked. "We can't have that."

Wade dealt him a dubious look that said he suspected Kirk was being sarcastic. "We want you to gather evidence that substantiates the Tengfeng family's underhandedness with us."

Kirk nodded. "I can do that. I'm not sure your boss wants to spend that kind of money." Kirk motioned to the marble and burlwood in the saloon.

Wade screwed up his face and bent over deprecatingly. "Money? Seriously?"

Kirk relaxed and stretched his arms along the back of the gold-silk divan. "Flat rate. My services are just ounces a day."

"Drugs?"

"South African one-ounce gold Krugerrands, three of them per day. Plus, expenses."

Wade spun on his heel and washed his hand down his face. From the sag in his shoulders, Kirk read he flummoxed the guy. Wade returned to Kirk, shaking his head, throwing up a hand. "Who the fuck do you think you are?"

Kirk eyed the half-moon camera in the ceiling and winked. *Well, here goes nothin,'* "I'm a SEAL." He let that pass without Wade's appreciation. "I'm a convicted killer." *Did he just flinch?* "I don't cast my pearls before swine." Kirk rose, smoothed his shirt in his waistband, and stepped toward the side deck.

Kirk's elation at not getting jumped fueled his casual stride toward exiting the yacht. As he reached for the gangway railing, an impeccably dressed Asian man in his thirties called out to him. "Mr. Roman?"

"I am." Kirk stood, feet shoulder-width apart, knees flexed, his hands at his side. "And you are?"

The man's voice was as smooth as his gait as he approached Kirk, his long fingers met and touched sequentially, tented in front of him. *Obsessive/compulsive disorder?* "I am Peng Huang. I've been observing your discussion with my employee."

Kirk cocked his head and removed his sunglasses, tapping the earpiece on his left hand. "Your employee is a poser. I am not. I don't suffer fools."

Peng's chin rose impudently. "Killers never do." A glimmer of a smile tilted Peng's mouth. "I see you and I are two of a kind."

Kirk gazed at Peng over his shoulder with an appraising look. "Then why do you need me?"

"I can't be everywhere, and those who need to be watched know my face."

Kirk acquiesced with a nod. "If your rival, what's his name? Tengfeng needs to be dealt with. I can handle that." He turned square into Peng. "I won't report to Wade."

Peng smirked. "No, I wouldn't expect you to. You report to me. Your proposal for payment is audacious. I like that. It is, of course, out of the question."

Kirk put on his sunglasses, smiled, and turned back toward the gangway. "Nice meeting you. Enjoy your time on the island." He headed off the yacht.

Peng moved rapidly, his hand shooting across Kirk's path. "Out of the question, however, there are other bold choices for payment."

Kirk lifted a brow. "Such as…"

Peng gestured him toward the yacht's stern and a staircase. "This is closer to heaven." *I do not believe heaven is a place you'll ever see.* Kirk followed Peng up into an elegant gambling salon. The poker table dominated the space. With exaggerated pride, Peng pressed a button on the wall, and the ceiling retracted, bathing the room in the bright Hawaiian sun. Peng stood; hands clasped in front of him. "Welcome to Seventh Heaven."

Kirk observed each machine and table with a casual expression. *How do you look past the number of women in every nook and cranny?* "I'm not a gambling man; how does this counter my proposal?"

Peng nodded toward the variety of games and women. "My guests often play for stocks, property, or sexual favors. We have men *and* women…"

"I'm happy for them. I trust gold." Kirk handed Peng a business card. "I've dealt with Oahu Gold and Silver from the day I landed on this island. Ask for Dennis."

Peng studied the card. "You are confident to arrive at our meeting with this card." Peng waved the card at Kirk.

"Would you hire an insecure agent? All my confidential transactions move across Dennis's desk."

Head down, Peng thumbed the edge of the business card. "Then we need to determine my expectations of your services."

Kirk raised a brow. "I thought you wanted me to follow and report on your competitor. What do you need now, another dealer?"

"You're being hired to follow a man highly trained in intelligence work." Peng almost sneered at Kirk. "If that were not the case, Wade could follow him."

Kirk nodded judiciously.

Head tilted; Peng studied him with a glint in his eye. "How can you say you don't gamble? My games are my most precious enterprise."

Kirk pressed harder. "Precious, you don't often hear that word in relation to business. It sounds as if you raised your skill to a thrill."

Peng's face shone. "Have you never experienced that surge of adrenaline when you risk everything and win?"

Kirk answered dryly. "I was a SEAL, remember? Gambling isn't a win in battle."

Peng looked down his nose. "So you say. Poker is life. Life with exceptional companions and top-shelf liquor."

"You must be constantly on the lookout for the next great competitor."

****

When Kirk pulled his phone out of the trunk, there were nine missed calls and texts from Jordan, Jax, and Hank. He grinned at the warm light of the late afternoon sun and thumbed a group text. "You better have a big spread for dinner. I'm famished. Home soon."

****

Kirk returned to Jax's estate. He honked the horn as he pulled the car under the porte-cochre and closed the dolphin gates. He laid his fingers on the keypad to enter the code, and the front door flew open. Jordan barreled into him. "I thought you'd never get home. Are you okay?" Her hands framed his face, then his shoulders, and traveled anywhere an injury could be inflicted.

"I sent you a text. I'm fine. I'm better than fine. I'm pumped." He punched one fist into his palm. "Let me get inside. You won't believe this clusterfuck." Kirk walked into the living room and bellowed. "Welcome friends, to the show that never fails to entertain—rich, crooked people!" Everyone followed Kirk into the kitchen. He regarded the empty island. "Didn't I text all of you that I was famished? What, do I have to play the spy and the food delivery guy, too?"

Hands on hips, Jordan shot him an indignant look. "Yes, Sire. We starved, waiting for you. Everyone, grab a plate." She placed the crockpot in the center of the island. Kameo grabbed the slider buns and Ava pulled out the tub of Hawaiian-style potato macaroni salad and a tray of cut fruit from the fridge.

Hank opened the beverage cooler and looked around. "It's after five, I deserve this after the stress of you being out of my sight all afternoon." He carried beers to the kitchen island, and the men claimed every bottle.

Jax filled a plate and perched on a barstool. After a long swig of beer, he gave a 'come on' hand gesture. "Get started."

Kirk piled his plate high with Kalua pork on slider rolls and swigged half a bottle of beer. Jax gestured again for his meeting's revelation. Famished, Kirk cleaned his plate before he pushed it back and dug into his cargo shorts pocket. Kirk pulled out a pack of index cards and his pen to begin writing highlights on each card. The group watched him sort them into hierarchies as he moved the cards into a different order before he cleared his throat and grinned confidently.

Hank chuckled. "Romeo, you are an analog guy in a digital world. Seriously, three by five cards?"

Kirk arched a brow. "I'm staying out of the matrix." The people around the table drew in a breath, and Kirk nodded. "If Peng was putting his eggs in Wade's basket, that gives you some idea of the cracks in his organization."

Hank sat back; arms crossed over his broad chest. "Duh!"

Jax scooped up more pork and impatiently shook his head. "What's he about?"

Kirk lowered his voice and turned the cards around for everyone to read. "I was ready to wipe my feet on Wade in three minutes. That conversation confirmed the entire yacht is wired with cameras and hot-and-cold-running women. At my first attempt to leave, the big man himself stopped me."

Jordan gulped her mouthful of food. "Peng?"

Kirk's brows drew up. "Yeah, according to him, we're brothers from another mother."

About to take another bite, Jordan halted, fork in the air. "Yeech."

"Peng is about five foot ten, athletic, quite an unusual haircut, a snappy dresser. With the bevy of female companionship on the yacht, he thinks he's all that." Kirk moved an index card to the top of the pile. I'll tell you what really flips his switch though, it's poker. We have ourselves a genuine player. More than the drugs and the girls, Peng loves the games. If we want an in, that's the avenue."

Hank raised his index finger. "So, why did he want to hire you?"

Kirk fished for a photo from the dossier he was given. "This is the fly in Peng's ointment, Syaoran 'Ronnie' Tengfeng."

Jax's head raised in recognition. "Wait, who? Ronnie Tengfeng?" Kirk nodded and turned the picture in his direction. Jax stared at the photo as he chewed. "You son of a bitch, bend over cause this time, it's my turn."

Ava's cheeks flushed, and Hank stifled his laughter. "What do you mean by that?"

Jax wiped his mouth with his napkin and shook his head. "Ronnie and I were on a joint military exercise. Each night, the officers had a friendly game of poker. It didn't matter who supplied the cards, Ronnie cleaned us out every damn night. I think the fucker counts cards." Ava sat with her mouth agape. Jax winced. "Sorry, ladies. He emptied my wallet, and I swore I'd learn to be a better card player before I sat at a table with him again."

Kirk shot his finger like a gun. "How well do you know Ronnie? Do you trust him?"

Jax shrugged. "He was a hell of an officer. Do you trust a card sharp? What are we talking about?"

Kirk winked. "Hank, how's your card playing?"

Ava's mouth dropped open. Hank chuckled. "I can represent. What are you thinking?"

Kirk smiled at the gathering around the table. "I think you're going to be Peng Huang's next opponent." Hank gestured his approval with his pipe and nodded. Kirk pulled out his phone and referenced a contact. "This guy is a tech wizard. He can make you an internet profile that says you are the next hot thing in poker tournaments. He'll hack into poker magazines…"

Ava gaped. "There are poker magazines? I lived in Las Vegas for ten years and never heard of them."

"There are poker magazines, internet ranking sites. By the time our guy is through, you'll swear Hank has a hot new career."

Ava frowned. "How will Hank explain he's suddenly got a place in that world?"

Hank stretched out his legs, cracked his neck, and grinned expansively. "I've been a General in the Air Force. I couldn't participate in tournaments, but now I'm retired and free to play anywhere. Turns out I have a mind for poker."

Jordan winced. "And they'll buy that?"

Jax raised a brow with a chuckle. "Have you seen the internet? All these people who come from nowhere and suddenly, they are the influencers?"

Hank sat pensively. "It's all in how I sell it. Tonight, you're sitting next to the Poker Beast of Bagram."

Kirk pulled out his next index card. "I wonder if we can pump up the volume by pitting Peng against Ronnie at a card table? According to Peng's intel, there should be time. Ronnie will arrive via his charter jet and sweep into his rented estate on the north shore. Peng's suspicious about the exact nature of his visit. Supposedly, he simply enjoys the island, but Peng's not buying it. He's not the most secure guy to begin with, and Ronnie is too powerful a player for his liking. There's quite a rivalry between their triads."

Jax nodded. "Most powerful families shield their sons from service. Not the Tengfeng family. They consider service an honor. A lot of them, like Ronnie, go to college in the United States and then into the military."

Hank cocked his head. "Sounds almost American."

Jax agreed. "Ronnie said, 'Why should the triads train their armaments dealers when military service would do a tighter job?'" He turned the beer bottle neck down into the bucket and opened another one. "Ronnie's family would jump at the chance to acquire Peng's territory."

****

When you're spending your time waiting on other people's schedules, the days drag. Hank came home late, or you could call it early in the morning, depending on your perspective. He quietly showered in the far bathroom so as not to disturb Ava. When he slipped into bed, he felt her comforting warmth and fell asleep within her arms.

At nine-fifty-five the next morning, Hank was startled awake. *When was the last time I slept till ten?* The condo was quiet. He rose and scratched all the usual body parts as he headed to the bathroom. When he flipped on the light, he swallowed hard. All of Ava's things were gone.

Was I so busy with Kingston Air yesterday that I missed the news that she was headed somewhere else for business? He checked his phone for messages, but there was nothing. *Why would she leave and not say goodbye?* A sliver of icy fear danced up his spine. Hank fell into a funk and moved mechanically as he prepared for his day.

In the kitchen, the stack of post-it notes, and the pen were left on the counter. Morosely, he placed them back on their tray. He gazed at the length of the kitchen counters, but no note.

Was I presumptuous? Did I say something to upset her? She wasn't kidnapped from our bed. Her things are gone and so is she. This is silly. I need to give her a call. The phone went directly to voicemail.

"Hi, this is Ava Hansen from Hau'oli Events. I'm making island magic for a valued client. Please leave your message and I'll return your call."

I hate voicemail. "Ava, this is Hank. Call me." Hank's phone beeped and showed an image of Sky at his front door. He hit a button and smiled. "Hey, Peanut, what's up?" *She's going to see right through me.*

Chapter Nine

He opened the door and triumphantly, Sky swept in. She held up two large quarts of ice cream. "With all this calamity, we haven't had the chance to sit down for our father-daughter ice cream break. I brought our favorites."

Hank's smile emerged. "Toasted coconut, pineapple whip, and macadamia chunk with fudge swirl."

Sky hugged her dad with the two containers out at her side. "I've missed you, Daddy… Stop whatever you're doing and let's gnosh."

While the early summer breeze swept over them, Sky's expression turned inquisitive. "What's Ava's favorite ice cream?"

"The subject never came up."

Sky sat and opened her container. "Well, go ask her. Maybe it's one of ours."

Head down over his treat, he spoke in barely a whisper, "She's not here."

"That's too bad." Sky dug into her sundae and halted. "Where is she?"

"I don't know." His tone was flat.

"What do you mean, you don't know? Isn't she in peril? You let her just go off on her own? Who's with her?"

Hank's hand crushed the napkins next to his spoon. "What was it you said to me once, 'I'm a grown-ass woman, I can take care of myself.'?"

Sky's head shook. "But did I? There was that mess with my professor… Dad, I'm serious. Where is she?"

Soberly, Hank took a deep breath and answered. "I had a late night with people from Kingston Air. When I came home, she was in bed. I tried not to wake her. I woke up, and she was gone. No note, no damn anything. I can't raise her on the phone. I think it's very inconsiderate."

Sky stopped eating and gawked. "Okay—"

He blurted over his daughter's reply. "It's not okay. All her things are gone."

Sky slid her hand across the table and patted her father's arm. "I know you and the Romans are helping her. Maybe she just had to change out of her clothes before she went to work."

Hank's gaze widened. "She could have woken me up. I'd go with her…"

Sky cocked her head. "Dad, maybe she is not used to having someone in her shadow. Maybe she'd rather do things on her own." Sky lifted her spoon. "Let's finish our empty calories and then you can check at her temporary office. I'd bet she's there."

****

The wheels of his new AMG E 53 Cabriolet squealed as Hank turned into the garage at Silver Seal. He caught a glimpse of Ava's shining blonde hair in the window of the office next door. Swinging the gearshift into park, he took the steps two at a time to get to her.

She buzzed him in. "Good morning, you were sleeping so soundly…"

He paced back and forth in front of her desk, running a hand through his hair in agitation. "You scared the hell out of me."

"What? Why?" She looked genuinely bemused.

"I can't believe you're sitting there with that smile on your face and not understanding why I'm upset." She folded her hands on the desk and cocked her head. "Why am I upset? I woke up. All your things were gone, no explanation. I tried to call and just got voicemail. You could have been dead on the side of the road." He wiped saliva from his lips. "Or worse."

She shook her head. "I left a note with those post-it notes on your counter, stuck it right on the freezer."

Hank felt foolish. "Oh." He turned away from her, head bowed, and when he faced her again, confessed, "I bought those damn things at a dollar store, and they don't stick worth crap."

"You thought I packed my things and left you?"

Hank's breathing hitched. "Well, yeah. I kind of did."

"No, I wasn't leaving you… it's just that I was so rattled when we left my place. I took all the wrong things." Ava's shoulders dropped. "But now that we're discussing this…"

Hank's posture stiffened. "Yes, and…" He stepped closer to her desk; his brows knitted.

"Well, it's just that I'm missing my place and my own things around me." Ava shrugged. "Do we still think I'm in imminent danger? Is it actually unsafe for me to go home?" She unclasped her hands and gestured with fingers spread. "I'm used to being alone."

Hank's expression was grim. "We have no way of knowing the peril you're in. Are you saying I'm not included in you being in your own place and around your own things?"

Ava rubbed at her forehead. "No, I'm not saying that at all. You are welcome to come over any time… but…"

Hank pivoted a quarter turn, his fists on his hips. "Let's have it."

"Hank, I know we met last year when we started emailing about Sky's wedding, but we met in person a week ago. No one is proposing permanence, so… aren't we getting too close too fast?" She stopped for a beat and winced. He didn't make a sound. "I mean, I'm beginning to feel absorbed into this huge thing…" She ended lamely with her arms out as if holding a huge awkward thing.

Hank searched within himself for their connection. Still posed before her, he turned on one foot and bowed his head. With a cleansing breath, he pivoted back to her. "I understand your hesitancy. Of course, I do. Under normal circumstances, we'd be dating, maybe having occasional sleepovers… but want it or not, we have a situation not only involving you but dozens of victimized women and men. Maybe hundreds of them. Not to mention drugs and guns." He wiped down his face with one hand, took another breath, and his voice gentled. "I'm an inside man on this takedown and although it wouldn't be good for me if Peng associated us, I want you safe, here. I'll tell you what, if it's feeling overwhelming staying with me, I have a spare bedroom. No hanky-panky. Or you can stay with Jax and Kameo…?"

"Look, General, I wasn't born yesterday. I've had to slug through things that would make your organized head spin." His lips drew straight, although he stayed silent. "I was under suspicion of offing my husband." Hank blinked hard. "That sonofabitch was right up there with Bernie Madoff. I went through five years looking over my shoulder." There was a beat of silence. "I want to be in my own place, with my own things, in my routine by myself."

Hank's nostrils flared. "Well, you can't be." He brooked no denial. "That's just it, you can't. I don't care if you were the button man for the Gottis."

She blinked hard and sat up straighter. "You truly believe it's still that dangerous?"

Hank slipped his hands into his pockets. "Have you paid Peng his $178,000.00?"

Ava covered her mouth and dropped back in her chair. She replied in a near whisper. "No."

Hank's lips were a thin line. "He undoubtedly hasn't forgotten about that."

Ava gave a wry smile. "The mob never does."

Hank nodded decisively. "So, what's it going to be, Jax and Kameo, with 4:30 AM boot camp, or me? I promise the new stove is coming next week."

Ava cracked a genuine smile and teased. "Oh, sure, that's what they all say."

Hank's shoulders relaxed. "I've been doing pretty well with your wok lessons, haven't I?" Ava stood and Hank held out his arms. "Get in here, Sunshine. You know I'm crazy about you."

She looked up at him with a wry smile. "Certifiable?"

He hugged her tighter. She pressed her cheek against his heart. "I'm getting tired of teriyaki. I think we should stop by my place and pick up my crock-pot."

He cuddled her. "And bring back the stuff you like." She nodded, and he walked her out with his arm around her shoulders. "I have a great recipe for pot roast. Excellent comfort food."

"What about the 'hanky-panky'?"

****

Across town, Jax got ready to carry out his portion of the mission. He readjusted the horn-rimmed eyeglasses on his face and smoothed back his longer than usual hair. *Darn curls.* The tony jewelry store was filled with tourists in search of inlaid opal, onyx, and mother-of-pearl fine jewelry. Jax hung back, afraid he would offend a customer who felt ignored. He dipped behind the curtain and hung around the goldsmith's bench. There he got the stink eye from the old man who laboriously toiled over a watch back that refused to pop off. The old man raised his head. "You new here?"

Jax shoved his hands into his pockets. "I'm a temp." The goldsmith shook his head and returned to prodding the watch back.

The front door's discreet chime rang, and there was Ronnie Tengfeng flanked by his ninja bodyguards, trailed by his wife and teenage daughter. The shop owner graciously took Mrs. Tengfeng aside and plied her with top-shelf Mai Tais. The teen, Li Na, hung close to her father in the hunt for the perfect fish pendant.

Jax and Haukea, the store owner's daughter, nodded at Ronnie before she launched into a friendly conversation with Li Na in Cantonese. As Ronnie hung back, uninterested in girl talk, Jax leaned across the case. He spoke quietly, "Sir, may I show you an heirloom plumeria watch that would complement the items your daughter seeks?" Ronnie's glance leapt to Jax's face. He stared hard as Jax sought to minimize his reaction with a discreet shake of his head.

Ronnie stood back and crossed his arms over his chest with a smirk. "You know my daughter's tastes?"

Jax reached for a key ring and met Ronnie's expression. "I know what Haukea is going to show her. Your daughter and she have been emailing back and forth."

Ronnie shook his head. "Once again, I've been played. My daughter mentioned the humuhumu fish pendant, and I see them looking at a tray of rings, earrings, and bracelets. My wife and the owner are enjoying her favorite sport, gossip."

Jax's brows waggled in jest. "If you'll permit me, I have something you need to see in the vault."

Ronnie dismissed his bodyguards with a look, as Jax walked to a large, ornately carved door, unlocked it, and ushered Ronnie back.

Once they were in the room of locked drawers with a narrow table and comfortable chairs, Ronnie punched at Jax's shoulder. "You've had a midlife crisis, or you've met a woman you need to keep in jewelry?"

Jax's brows drew together, and they began their greeting ritual of a couple of half-nelsons and a slap on the back. Jax slipped out of Ronnie's grasp. "Ten Fingers, you have an admirer who's put you under surveillance."

Ronnie walked around the large vault, straightening his clothing. "If I didn't, I must not be making enough waves. What brings the US Navy into this?"

Jax shook his head. "Not the Navy, in fact, not the US government in any way. I need to make that clear."

Ronnie sniffed. "Really? Why is that?" He examined his manicure.

"Peng Huang has decided you are a threat. He hired my dad to follow you and frame you in a compromising position."

"Did he, now?" Ronnie's smile developed as if Peng's attention was a compliment. The smile morphed to pursed lips and an expression of curiosity.

"This is your opportunity to put your foot on his neck, send him back to China, and take over his territory."

Ronnie frowned. "We handle gambling and the companionship of that lifestyle. I don't want Peng's territory. His triad runs guns, human trafficking, and drugs. I want no part of that."

"We don't either. We'd love to put Peng and his family out of business permanently. Unfortunately, his father is the ambassador of the People's Republic, and diplomatic immunity has kept his faction in business. The government can't touch him. However, I represent a group of interested citizens with a certain set of skills."

Ronnie snapped his fingers. "You've been watching too many movies, Flash…"

"Oh, Ronnie, this is real. We have reason to be displeased with Mr. Huang and his enterprises. This plan will get you gambling in the state of Hawaii. It comes with the opportunity to run a quintessential stable of willing and well-compensated professional women and men who keep your gamblers company."

Ronnie's gaze narrowed as his lips drew up in a winning smile. "You, dog. You offer me this after I emptied your wallet in Seoul?"

Jax removed his bothersome glasses and stuck them in his Aloha shirt pocket. "I'd have spent that money on roses and whiskey, anyway. Your family is held in high esteem. Why are the Huangs diplomats? They need to be recalled. Back to my offer. What do you think?"

"I concur. But come clean, Flash. Why are you involved?"

Jax sobered. "Huang is an arrogant little snot. A playground bully. He's put a good friend of ours out of business for pure meanness. But more than that… he's dealing in human misery. The people he traffics are not willing, far from it. His Fentanyl-laced drugs are killing people."

Ronnie's irritation piqued. "Peng is an arrogant stain on my people. He's a winner take all predator."

"That's diplomatic." Jax laughed and leaned across the table, pointing out to the jewelry store. "Look at your beautiful wife and daughter. If someone sullied them, what would you do?"

Ronnie's face became a stony mask, and he drilled his index finger on the table. "I'd take him down."

Jax leaned toward Ronnie across the table. "To do this right, we need your help."

****

"I am *not* moving off this chaise." A naked Hank spooned to a gloriously nude Ava on the lanai.

She snuggled into his embrace as she reached back and trailed fingernails up and down his thigh. "What are you doing to me? I'm supposed to be working on an event budget." A tourist helicopter flew over the Waikiki skyline and circled the canal. "You don't suppose the tourists have binoculars in those helicopters, do you?"

Hank scratched at his chest and wiped at their shared perspiration. "If they do, smile. I've got something to wave at them!"

His breath caught the cool sweat on her neck, and she quivered closer to him, covering his groin.

Her eyes narrowed. "No, you don't." She melted at the sight of her man in his post-coital bliss. "I'm glad we've had this day without a glitch, without an emergency call."

They got off the chaise and returned to the bedroom. After a quick shower, Ava walked from the bath in her robe, towel-drying her hair. She spied Hank nosing around the monogrammed Queen's wardrobe trunk. "Where did you get that? That's a gorgeous piece of vintage Louis Vuitton luggage."

"Jordan left this to me as a housewarming gift. Personally, I think it was too heavy for her to move." Hank rocked the full-size wardrobe trunk that stood on end in the far corner of his bedroom. "It's a high-end plant stand." He chuckled. "I heard it has a great provenance."

Ava tilted her head. "Well, I guess a Louis Vuitton trunk is worth a ten-dollar word for origin. So, spill, where's it from?"

Hank slapped his thigh and laughed. "This apartment was famous. Kirk got involved with an unsavory woman named LaDonna, who vented her jealousy on Jordan and Kameo. She was a little dangerous… the head of a drug cartel from Mexico. Want to hear the rest of the story?"

Ava shimmied her shoulders and cooed. "You've got me interested now, big boy."

Hank's gaze traveled to the lanai and back to the trunk. "You don't believe in ghosts, do you?"

Ava sobered. "There's not a body in it, is there?"

Hank shrugged casually. "Not as far as we know. But one and a half murders happened in the living room."

Ava's gaze narrowed. "One and a half?"

"From the story Jordan told me, LaDonna killed a dirty cop in the living room. She tried to kill Jordan and Kameo, they fought for their lives, and LaDonna met the effects of gravity when you go over the lanai railing. When it was over, our gals wanted their pound of flesh."

Ava shivered. "Now you have to tell the end."

"Jordan picked up a key ring from LaDonna's purse with a storage unit tag. Then they did some storage unit shopping."

Ava fell back into the chair and giggled. "I love storage unit auctions. Was Jordan acting legally?"

Hank shrugged. "Our friends were owed far more for their pain and suffering." He continued, "Kameo found a rack of gowns and suits she donated to her medical center's charity." Ava nodded. "Kirk threw a fit that Jordan insisted on taking this trunk. He said it was the ugliest thing he'd ever seen."

"Did she ever open it? What if there is a body inside? Or drugs…. Open it, see what's in there."

Chapter Ten

The trunk keys hung in a pouch attached to the handle. Hank moved the silk plant onto the floor, unlocked it, and spread the trunk open like a book. It stood a little over four feet tall and two feet deep. When it pivoted open, there were seven drawers on one side.

"Knowing LaDonna, it's stuffed with ammo."

Ava frowned. "You think?" She moved to Hank's side. "Your gift, your discovery." He stood over the top drawer and drew it open. "What…? What…? What is it?"

Hank whistled. "I think I know what this is." They stared at bands of one-hundred-dollar bills in ten-thousand-dollar increments.

Ava's eyes grew wide. "How do you like the ugly luggage now?"

Hank pumped his fist in victory. "I can't freaking believe this."

They fanned a stack of bills at each other. "Check the other drawers." She knelt beside Hank, and each drawer revealed more well-used cash. "Mother of God."

He sat back on his heels and shook his head. "My housewarming gift was a private ATM."

Ava slid her stack back into the drawer. "Was that woman involved in counterfeiting?"

Hank shrugged, and both hands flew out in surrender. "She was the queen of a drug cartel; this… is… real, and our solution to floating me as a whale."

Ava's eyes narrowed. "I beg your pardon?"

Hank smiled expansively. "We were going to sell me as a whale for a high-stakes poker game on Peng's boat, but none of us had access to even counterfeit cash. Kirk and Jax talked about a line of credit on the gym…"

Ava sobered. "They'd gamble their business to help me?"

Hank walked to the beverage station in the bedroom and poured a drink for each of them. "It's like this… Ava, you mentioned being caught up in this 'thing.' We're a family, now you're part of it. So, let's call Kirk and Jordan down here and gloat about what they had under their noses.

****

Kirk strolled up the gangway, feeling flush, knowing that the con was set. *If you have to march through hell, march as if you own the place.* When the gorilla twins approached Kirk, Peng stepped from the aft salon and held up a halting hand. "Good afternoon, Mr. Roman. Come with me. As Kirk followed Peng, he caught Wade disappearing back into the central saloon.

Peng sat on the luxuriously upholstered bow-deck couch as a naked woman swam in the pool before him. *I'll bet she is not his wife.* For one wild moment, Kirk wondered if she was there as an art installation. *Perhaps they change swimmers every eight hours?*

Peng gestured to a chair, and Kirk pulled up the thighs of his dress trousers as he sat. With Peng's nod and an imperious wave, the athletic beauty vaulted from the pool and walked away dripping.

"Tasmanian Rain, Mr. Roman?" A Waterford ice bucket sat with an artful bottle and two rocks glasses.

"Excuse me?"

"It is indeed rainwater from Tasmania. You must try it. It's all you'll want in water." Peng extended the glass proudly.

Kirk nodded and accepted the glass. Peng raised his glass in a toast, and when Kirk swallowed, he hid his astonishment that it was, indeed, water. "That's…" Kirk searched for a word. "… zesty." Kirk winked and sat down the glass. "While we're riding that high, let me fill you in on Mr. Tengfeng."

"Please do."

Kirk pulled a small Moleskin notebook from his breast pocket and reviewed his writing before looking up. He gestured to the ship. "Do you ever move this thing?"

Peng's gaze narrowed. "What do you mean?"

"Well, I've scoped out the place our friend frequents, and it's just around the coast. I didn't know a place like that existed, and I've lived here for twenty-plus years." Peng paced the deck, hitching his linen trouser waistband. "But you know, this ship is a bit showy for spycraft. Got anything we could take out for a couple of hours?"

"Let me order out the launch." Peng picked up the telephone intercom. "Make ready the Evening Star." He hung up the phone and headed toward the stairs. Kirk fell into step behind the man, absorbing every detail below deck. When they arrived in the garage, they passed a pair of jet skis and an assortment of water toys. The launch sat chugging, waiting for them to board as a man in class B whites bowed to them, and left. "Will you do the honors?"

Kirk stood silent for a blessed moment. *In my life, I never expected to pilot a launch out of the hull of a superyacht.* Kirk looked over his shoulder at Peng, already seated. "All lines cast?" Peng looked around imperiously and shrugged. *We'll find out when the boat rips out its mooring.* Kirk entered the ocean resort's location into the navigation system, shifted forward, and at idle speed moved away from The Vesper.

The small craft moved parallel to the island's southern coastline until they approached Barber's Point Harbor. Kirk shifted into idle and turned off the launch. Peng's relaxed posture abruptly changed. "Why are we stopping? I see no resort."

Kirk leaned back on the gunwale and took out his notebook. "It's private out here; I like it like that." Peng paced the small deck. "So, here we go… Your man Ronnie is one odd duck. He comes into town, takes his wife and daughter to a series of jewelry stores and fashion houses. Then he brings in a surfing coach, charters a snorkeling tour, and buys out a night at Chef Hilo's. He flew in the Jonas Brothers for his daughter's eighteenth birthday. This has been a family-oriented trip."

Peng's lips curled in derision. "This is not what I paid you for."

Kirk looked at a seabird circling above and adjusted his sunglasses. "You're paying me to catch him doing something. You are not paying for me to plan it." Peng harrumphed. "But all is not lost. Mr. Tengfeng's wife and daughter are leaving on Monday for Miami. From there, Nova University in Fort Lauderdale, where the missus outfits the daughter's apartment before school starts in the fall. Lots of mommy-daughter time so daddy can play."

Peng's flat expression brightened. "How long?"

"Long enough. The missus didn't schedule a return flight. She could be returning directly to China from there. Ears to the ground say Mr. Tengfeng has a fascination with this resort." Kirk fired the ignition and goosed the throttle. Peng flew back into a seat and held on. "Mind your footing."

They bounced on the waves past Ko Olina Beach, the lagoon, and a string of traditional timeshare resorts. As they approached a pink castle rising out of the ocean in Milo Bay, Peng's attention drilled on what looked like an ode to Hearst's San Simeon. Spanish Renaissance in style with Gothic influences, it was a massive castle on pilings driven into the water's bedrock. Kirk swung the boat around in a broad circle and pointed the bow straight at the rosy fortress. "Ever been there?"

Peng caught up a micro pair of binoculars. "What is this place?"

Kirk nodded appraisingly. "Not listed on any tourist site, not ranked by Forbes. Never advertised anywhere. It's as private as The Bohemian Grove."

"And Tengfeng comes here?" He gestured at the architecture, nonplussed. "What does he do here?"

"Nobody knows." Kirk lifted a brow. "It can't be good, or people would talk about it."

"How do I get in?" Peng leaned on the gunwales toward the resort. "I, I want to go there." He pounded his chest like Celine Dionne.

Kirk shook his head. "All my research points me toward a company in Los Angeles, and my calls were not returned. Arrival is by helicopter and launch between dusk and dawn."

Peng stood and folded his arms imperiously across his chest. "They'll return my calls."

Kirk leaned casually against the Bimini top and regarded the sea birds and the dolphins. "You can try…"

"I have what they want." Peng looked down his nose and snorted.

"How do you know?"

"I know… take me home."

****

Hank and Ava were learning how to be a couple and still be in separate rooms of his condo. After dinner and a soothing soak, Ava sought a cup of tea. Approaching the kitchen, she caught the faint scent of pipe tobacco from the lanai. She heard the sound of shuffling cards. It was Hank. He sat, resolute, with the pipe between his teeth as he shuffled for the desired card.

Ava smiled at the memory of watching The Sting and how the man practiced stacking the deck. She peeked out at the lanai. "Can I make you something?"

He kept shuffling, his concentration blocking her question. She slipped silently outside and stood behind him, watching, and realizing he was oblivious to the world. She reached around and stroked his cheek. "You're so handsome in the sunset."

111

Cards flew out of his hands, his pipe bounced sparks, and his hulking frame jolted in the chair. "George Patton's nuts." He grabbed at the flying cards.

Ava jumped back and smirked. "I'm sorry. I thought you heard me."

"It's okay. I didn't need those last ten years, anyway."

"What are you doing? Practicing to become a whale? You can't stack the deck; they frown on that."

****

Jordan paced the length of the lanai, a bag of frozen blueberries in one hand as she shoved them into her mouth one at a time. She chewed as she watched Kirk shave and prepare for his night of espionage. "How do you know this guy? He's a kid; he looks younger than Jax. Dang, barely older than Conner." She hovered over Kirk's smartphone at an image of a debonair young man with a thousand-dollar haircut and whiskey-colored eyes. "Hank is going, too?"

Kirk nodded as he strode toward her, took the bag out of her hands, and threaded his fingers with hers. "Jordie, Evan Silver vouches for Mr. Hiatt." He nodded toward the image on the phone. "I'm quoting him now; you can't have a better man in your corner. Stop worrying." Kirk drew her back into the bedroom while he finished dressing. He stepped into his shoes, dropped his wallet into his pocket, and put on his ring and watch. "The helicopter will be here shortly. So nice of you to pick a building with a helipad." He picked up his phone as his security system announced Hank at the front door.

Jordan bit at a hangnail. "Just don't bring the fight back here. The fish tank is just the way I want it."

"You worry too much. This is just an evening to talk, lay some groundwork."

112

Before Jordan could cook up more objections, an ebony helicopter shot silently over the Ala Wai Canal, circled the building, and rose to land on the roof. "I didn't even hear that."

Kirk's phone buzzed in his pants. "That's my ride up there. Hank's at the front door. We'll be back in a couple of hours." He hugged her tightly and pressed a kiss on her gaping mouth. "Don't wait up."

As Kirk headed out the front door to meet Hank, Jordan headed back to the lanai to watch the silent craft fly into the night. *That's just weird.*

****

The men settled into the fine leather of the sleek helicopter's interior. Fitting on headsets without instruction, they answered the pilot's polite inquiry.

"Are you comfortable, gentlemen? Do you have any questions?"

Hank spoke for both of them. "All aces here, Captain."

"Very well, sir, our flight time is approximately ten minutes."

By Hank's watch, it was more like eight minutes and thirty seconds when they landed. The resort was so spacious that the heliport sat in the center of the castle's massive roof. The valet was dressed in a stylish Aloha shirt in the tones of the castle. He opened the Airbus's door, and they stepped down. The man gestured to a small building in the corner and spoke over the sound of the slowing rotors. "Welcome to Mele Lani, gentlemen. This way to Mr. Hiatt's private elevator."

They smoothed their hair back from the brisk breeze before the elevator doors closed. Alone in the glass and hammered copper elevator, traditional island music played softly as the rising moonlight shone over the waves. When the elevator car slipped beneath the waterline, the lights dimmed to luminescent red, and the thrum of a human heartbeat resonated.

113

Hank shivered and shook off the eerie feeling. "Well, you don't hear that every day." Although Kirk made no reply, Hank read his friend's unease. The slow ride treated them to the sight of nocturnal sea life wandering through what was perhaps a protected environment.

"I've snorkeled this entire island and never seen this assortment together. Magnificent. I have to bring Jordan here." Kirk's attitude brightened.

Hank nodded. "Yeah, Jordan has some great aquariums. This guy lives within an aquarium."

They left the elevator car and entered a massive glass-walled room supported by Italianate pillars. The spectacle of the room's peaceful décor awed them. Their attentions were drawn to the expanse of the living sea surrounding a room of sand-toned wood floors. Silk pillows in brilliant undersea colors invited them to relax on the long, low furniture. No need for art. Simply the muted downlighting emphasized the languid sea life around them.

Out of an unseen corner, a smooth-voiced, trim man emerged to greet them. "Good evening, Mr. Roman, General Kingston. Welcome to my home, away from home." He sounded like he had secrets to tell. Hank turned abruptly to meet the man.

The business executive, whose photo was in Kirk's email, appeared youthful, although his eyes carried a worldly mien. He nodded at them and rolled on the balls of his bare feet before he gracefully strode to shake their hands. Dressed casually in parchment-colored, fine-linen slacks and a tailored Aloha shirt, he extended a hand. "Rick Hiatt. Evan speaks highly of both of you. May I offer you sake? It's brewed especially for Mele Lani."

Hank held Haitt's hand a second longer than expected, nodded, and slipped his hand back into his trouser pocket. "Proprietary sake sounds wonderful."

Hiatt held up a torch cigar lighter and stood at the bar. "Chilled or warmed?"

The men found themselves drawn to the simply crafted bar area, and the cobalt-blue antique sake warmer. Hiatt performed the warming ritual respectfully. "I've always preferred my sake warmed; it enhances the delicate aroma."

The men nodded, coming to grips with the idea of this stranger's hospitality in such extraordinary surroundings. The fish oh'd at them from all around the room. As Hiatt warmed the sake, he glanced over his shoulder. "Oh, they do watch us. Sometimes, we are the entertainment."

Kirk gestured at the windows. "It seems fair. We watch them often enough. My wife is quite a devotee of aquariums and snorkeling. If I brought her here, she'd expect me to build something like this for her."

"You must bring her." Hiatt cocked a brow and gestured to the room. "The place is deserted during the day; the fish are lonely."

Hank, used to seeing sheik's wealth and refinement, scrutinized Hiatt, and his environment. *I can't even imagine how many billions went into this.*

Kirk stepped closer to the window, where a ray slipped by. "Evan told me you're a man of justice and action." Kirk turned back to face Hiatt.

"In today's society, the wheels of justice often grind up the poor, leaving the wealthy and privileged criminals untouched." Hiatt's brow rose, and he drew in a deep breath. With a tilt of his head, he continued his task. "I support a system of fair and swift justice."

Hank's hands delved into his pockets as he strolled the room and thought about this young billionaire's words. "Mr. Hiatt, am I bunking up with an anarchist?"

Hiatt's boyish side erupted and with a broad smile, he answered. "Sir, you are, indeed, a military man. No, I do not espouse anarchy. I'm here to assist you in shining a light on the guilty." His chin tucked for a second, and when he straightened up, his whiskey-colored eyes gleamed. "This is about that malignant entity sweeping these shores."

Hank's gaze met Hiatt's. "'Malignant' truly is an apt word for Peng Huang and his daddy's triad. They don't bother you out here, do they?"

"I've sheltered a few refugees from his abuse. Gentlemen, you must understand a resort of this nature," he gestured upward. "Relies on safe and sane consensual activities."

Kirk brushed at his bottom lip. "'Safe and sane consensual activities?'" He exchanged a look with Hank.

Hiatt's lips curled in a sly grin as he checked the temperature and dispensed sake in the most translucent cups Hank had ever seen. As he accepted the eggshell-shaped cup, he worried his grasp would shatter the delicate piece.

Hiatt held his cup aloft. "Kanpai!"

Hank and Kirk echoed the salute. Hank still wondered *what the hell does Hiatt mean by 'safe and sane consensual activities?'*

Hiatt waited as they savored the sake. As casually as if he were asking their preferences for coffee or tea, he inquired. "How comfortable are you with erotic practices of roleplaying involving bondage, discipline, and dominance?"

Kirk's throat tightened. He smiled and drained his cup. "I was in the Navy, served in Asia. I've been a few places and seen a few things."

Hiatt nodded. "That scratches the surface. We thrust a little deeper, our clientele demands it. We provide a safe place for sexual expression."

Hank's posture stiffened as he held out his cup with both hands. "'Sexual expression…?'"

Hiatt refilled their cups and returned to sit across from them. "Our organization supports our clients in expressing themselves in whatever way they are most comfortable." No longer holding a cup, his graceful fingers played with the yellow gold, and emerald heraldic ring on his right hand. Hank noticed Hiatt wore a wide, gold Celtic wedding band. "Have you, for instance, ever fantasized about being the sheriff and rescuing your saloon girl from a dastardly bad guy…?" Hank's lips curled upward, and his face flushed. Hiatt paused. "Have I embarrassed you?"

Hank full-out chuckled. "I'm beating back the image of the cowboy and the saloon girl. My daughter is about to marry Kirk's youngest son who is from Texas."

Kirk and Hank exchanged a flinch. "Although he's an adult, I need brain bleach to keep the images out of my head. He and his young lady are very happy…"

The lights danced in Hiatt's eyes. "Then they might enjoy our frontier room. But I digress. Evan said you needed my help, and I doubt your son and his lady need any inspiration." Hiatt's head dropped back, his eyes closed, and he smirked. "Oh, love, a madness most discreet."

Kirk wagged a finger at Hiatt. "Not at their age… But yes, Evan did mention you are the right man to have in our corner. I took the liberty of boating Peng Huang past this resort. As I hoped, he can't stand that a mystery is beyond his grasp."

Hiatt relaxed in his leather chair, his hands resting on its arms as he absorbed Kirk's proposal.

****

After an hour or so of discussion, timelines, and plotting, Rick Hiatt's hands unfolded from his lap. "Absolutely, General Kingston,

117

you may consider our resort your own." Hiatt picked up the delicate cups. "Perhaps the last of this bottle?" While he poured, his smile warmed. "Mr. Roman, when would you like to bring your wife? You mentioned a son. Do you have other adult children? Mi castle, es su castle." He stroked the front of his colorful Aloha shirt. "Like the shirt? This green is the color of my wife's eyes. I'll make sure Anna is here when you visit. She loves visitors."

****

Kirk slept on his discovery of the pink palace of pleasure. In the morning, to flat out tease him, Kirk baited Peng. The phone rang once, and Peng answered. "You did not check in last night."

Kirk yawned and stretched, making sure the phone speaker caught the sound of bedsheets. "I was out last night." Kirk walked into the bathroom and needlessly flushed the toilet. He hit the sink faucet and began his game.

Peng's voice vibrated with outrage. "I don't pay you to be busy."

Kirk snorted. "So far, my goldsmith says you haven't paid me at all."

"Is that what this is about?"

Kirk turned on his sonic toothbrush and let it buzz. "I'm not doing this for my health. I have news you can use, but not until I see a receipt of deposit into my gold account."

"Hold on…"

Kirk took the time to brush his teeth and floss. He took extra care to trim his nose hairs. *This might be a while.* Kirk's phone buzzed receipt of a purchase confirmation in his name.

Peng inquired. "Do you see the transaction?"

"Yes, thank you." Kirk's voice was cool. "Are you sitting down? I hope you're not distracted by a naked swimmer."

Peng harrumphed. Kirk drew out his words. "I have the resort owner's name. Turns out, he's one of my clients at my fitness center. And the best news?"

Peng interrupted. "Yes, what?"

"He's the epitome of discretion."

Peng spat back. "That's good news?"

Kirk winked at himself in the bathroom mirror. "He's looking for a game, high-stakes poker. He loves the game, it's all he goes on about. I can't imagine he's particularly good at it. He's got no poker face. He and Ronnie Tengfeng are tight. But he won't talk to me about the resort.

Peng exploded. "He's tight with Ronnie? Why? How?"

Kirk made his voice nonchalant as he mugged in the mirror. "It's my understanding that Ronnie will be staying at the pink palace while the Mrs. is in Florida."

Peng was hot. "You have got to get me an invitation to that resort."

An evil side of Kirk emerged on the phone. "Well, there are initiation fees. You have to be recommended… They do background checks." Peng was silent for a long moment. "And…there are rumors the initial buy-in is said to be close to seven figures."

"If Ronnie Tengfeng can pass the background check and raise the money, so can I."

Kirk shot a finger gun at himself in the mirror and then placed both hands over his heart with an expression of anguish. He conceded mildly. "Well, we'll see."

Peng ranted. "Invite the resort owner to my boat tonight."

Kirk's eyes danced. "What? Do you think you'll serve him a few drinks…" Kirk sniffed and shrugged. "And after a few rounds of cards, you'll just wrangle an invitation?"

Peng barked. "I'll win an invitation."

Kirk nodded smugly. "That might be a possibility. Let me check with him about tonight." Peng ended the call and Kirk looked at the silent phone. *Asshole.*

****

Hank smiled the smile of an about-to-be satisfied man. Ava, dressed in red brocade, leaned on the piano as he threw open the barroom's swinging doors. The music stopped and men gaped at his ten-gallon hat and silver spurs. His gun belt slung low over his hips, hinting at the weight of his pistols. There she was, Miss Ava, biting her bottom lip as he ambled across the dusty wood floors.

She crossed the distance in the room's dead silence, her ruby earrings sparkling in the candlelight. She sidled up to him, purring. "It's so nice to see you're alive, Sheriff. I was terrified those varmints would outgun you and we would never share this again." She took off his hat and respectfully placed it on the bar. Then she caught him by the ears and delivered his lips to her ample bosom. "Are you hungry, Sheriff?" She released his head and ran her tongue over her top lip. "Cause I've got quite an appetite for you." She caught the steel in his jeans and fluttered her lashes at his length.

"Oh, my, Miss Ava, you are hungry." He nodded agreeably as he took her hand and followed her to the winding staircase.

"I want to take you higher…"

He frowned down at the cowpokes at the bar, who thumped their beer mugs for attention. *Sonnofabitch.* The thumping continued until Ava, in bed next to him, squealed, "What's happening?"

Chapter Eleven

Hank shook himself awake. "What?"

"Somebody's pounding on the door. What time is it?" She threw off the sheets to slide into her robe.

Hank looked at the clock. 6:05 AM. *Sonnofabitch.* "I recognize that knock." He picked up his phone and, seeing Kirk at his front door, Hank walked naked to the door and yanked it open. "What the fuck do you want, Romeo?"

Kirk raised a brow at Ava and with an enormous smile said, "Peng's champing at the bit to get the resort owner into the Seventh Heaven game. We will naturally disappoint him today. You're busy."

Ava and Hank looked at each other. Hank nodded. "Yeah."

"We need to plant a transmitter in Seventh Heaven so Jax can tap into the closed-circuit system and read the cards. I'm thinking our little event planner here must know the best place to get a big-ass floral arrangement that I can deliver with your apologies." He smirked. "I'm thinking one of those huge arrangements of baboon dicks."

Ava's hand flew to her mouth to hide her laugh. "Anthuriums?"

Kirk shot a finger at her. "Yeah and throw in a couple of bird of paradise blooms. It's got to be so huge that once I put it where I want it, nobody moves it."

Ava grinned. "Sure, I can do that!"

Hank wrapped an arm around her. "I guess we'd better count out the cash. Looks like I'll be playing cards tomorrow night."

Ave's hand flew to her chest. "Kirk, what's the dress code? I know these games are usually formal dress."

Hank's gaze darted from Ava to Kirk. "Can't wear my dress blues." He smiled. "Miss Ava, I guess I'd better find me a fancy tux, pronto."

****

Kirk slumped under the weight of the ridiculous floral arrangement as he trod up the gangway. Once on deck, he stopped, expecting the gorilla twins to meet him. When a sultry woman clad in a barely there chiffon wrap met him, she smiled. "Ohh, that's such a suggestive arrangement. Don't you think the bird of paradise is so… vaginal?"

Kirk hooked a look around the arrangement and deadpanned. "I'm just the delivery boy."

"Oh, is this for Bao-Bao?"

Kirk raised a brow. "Sure, who's Bao-Bao?"

Hovering over the anthuriums, she ran a long fingernail over the prominent, yellow spadix protruding from the carmine-red spathe. "This is so… virile. Clearly, this arrangement is meant for love."

Kirk shrugged. "How about you get Bao-Bao down here? This is for him." *I'm about to herniate myself.* He looked into the saloon expectantly, as his feet squared beneath his shoulders.

Peng descended the stairs curiously. "Mr. Roman, do you bear good news?"

Kirk hitched the plant to his hip and shrugged. "Mr. Huang, your guest sends regrets for tonight. He has another engagement. He insisted I bring this eighty-pound pot of baboon dicks and vaginal flowers," Kirk nodded at the woman hanging on Peng's arm, "to you for Seventh Heaven. What do you say? Can I cart this up there?"

Peng's expression brightened. "Of course, Mr. Roman."

With each step, Kirk cursed himself for suggesting such a ridiculous gift. Peng never cracked a smile. When Kirk arrived, there were red-coated staff setting up long buffet tables to precise specifications. At the poker table, other staff brushed the felt and spaced the chairs.

Kirk was grateful the floral arrangement contained a transmitter that Hank would engage when he arrived tomorrow. As he sat the pot on a permanent table in the corner of the room, his instincts were born out. A serious-faced flunky waved a wand over the three and a half feet of flora and nodded to Peng. Peng shrugged. "I cannot be too careful."

Backing away from the arrangement and dusting off his hands, Kirk slanted Peng a wry smile. "Turns out these suggestive flowers are more appropriate than you know. Rumor has it the pink palace is a sex club."

Peng's brows rose into his hairline. "Really? How interesting."

Kirk waved a finger at the arrangement. "Oh, yeah, they've got these damn things everywhere. Anyway, your guy will be here tomorrow night."

****

The morning of Kirk and Hank's trip to Seventh Heaven, Kirk paid special attention to his workout. He sparred with Conner in the empty mat room. Pinning him several times before taking mercy on the kid, Conner groused. "It's not fair. I don't have full strength in my right shoulder."

Kirk dismissed his cry. "I spent a month teaching you compensatory strategies. You just can't beat the old man."

Conner wiped the sweat off his brow. "Maybe I just don't want to embarrass you."

Disengaging from the grappling, Kirk grabbed a towel and wiped his face. "You need to come out of the gate at one hundred percent. You need to mean it. Because the day you'll need to win that fight, eighty percent isn't going to get it."

Conner stretched out his good arm. "What's all this talk about winning a fight? Even Jax is on me about being full out. Out of the

123

blue, you and Hank are MIA. When you are here, it's about defense like this. Who are we going to war against?"

Kirk thought about that and took a stance for Conner to charge. "You just worry about setting up your part of Kingston Air."

Conner took his position but relaxed his stance when Hank and Ava waved from the other side of the glass wall. "Oh, here we go. You two are about to disappear again."

Hank held the door open for Ava. "Who's disappearing? She smiled broadly at the shopping bags from Neiman Marcus. "He can't disappear until we get the altered tux. But we have all the other goodies."

Conner peered into the bag. "Hank, Ralph Lauren? You know the wedding isn't that formal…" He caught the shoe bag. "Nine hundred dollars for shoes?" Connor's jaw froze open. "Are you going to wear these with your pilot's uniform?"

"He could." Ava took obvious pride in holding open the bag to Kirk. "I think we caught the style just as it came in the store. No one else is wearing this yet."

Kirk smirked. "I'll bet Teflon is happy he found a crate of cash…"

"Trunk, Kirk. It's a Louis Vuitton trunk," Ava corrected.

Kirk threw out his hands to the side and scoffed. "A box by any other name could still carry cash." He regarded Hank. "When will your suit be ready?

Hank stood tall. "You mean my timeless and classic Lauren Purple-Label Douglas tux?"

Kirk caught the long register receipt from Neiman Marcus. "No, I mean your thirty-five hundred dollars 'wear it till you die' suit."

Hank waved off his friend's comments. "I wanted to check in with you. I think we should use Hiatt's Eurocopter."

Conner's ears pricked up. "Eurocopter? The five-bladed one you can't hear. Damn, I want to be with you guys. You have all the fun."

Kirk nodded at Hank. "Yeah, I'll call Hiatt about that. You get home and get in the zone for tonight."

Hank nodded. "By twenty-thirty, I'll be Cary Grant. Who will you be, Justin Bieber?"

Conner skirted the conversation circle. "Where are you guys going? First, it's talk about survival, now tuxedos and silent helicopters. Who are you, Austin Powers?"

Kirk turned to Conner and smirked. "Oh, behave. Make sure you cover that body-sculpting class tonight."

Ava gathered the bags from the men. "My service is delivering the tux to Hank's in the next couple of hours. We'll be on our way."

As Hank and Ava made their goodbyes and headed home, Conner would not shut up about the Eurocopter. Kirk slanted him a look. "If you are a good son, I might ask if you and Sky can be flown from the wedding reception in it." With that, he turned and headed for his office.

****

Once Hank was back home, the nerves hit. Looking at the tres-chic items of the wardrobe they'd bought, the reality of what could go wrong was a gut punch. Hank ran a hand through his hair. "What if that damn thing doesn't transmit and Jax can't see everyone else's hands?"

Ava shrugged. "Well, then, Peng might not think you were a world-class poker player, but they'll love you for your money. Besides, isn't Peng half-hooked on the kinky resort idea? Stop worrying. You could play Old Maid and he'd kiss your ass to win your invitation."

Hank laughed. "And he's going to have to work hard to do that."

125

Ava offered. "Perhaps a pot of calming tea?" Hank shook his head. "A drink?" Hank frowned. Ava brightened. "I just remembered a bachelor party I catered. They were getting ready to do some heavy drinking. I suggested a menu of salmon, asparagus, and a dessert of Greek yogurt with fruits high in potassium."

Hank cocked his head. "Why?"

"These are all the foods to prepare your body for alcohol. They combat dehydration and slow alcohol absorption. I'll get right on that."

As excited as Ava was, Hank needed a nap.

****

Try as he might, the barroom dream wouldn't pick up where Kirk interrupted Hank. He summoned all his best relaxation techniques and before he knew it, Ava was there sitting on the bedside. "Hey, handsome, time to rise and shine. Your tux is here."

Hank growled as he caught Ava around the waist and rolled her onto the bed. "How about a kiss for luck?"

Ava's gaze met his and, wordlessly, she surrendered to him for all kinds of luck. She wrestled out of his embrace and began removing articles of clothing as she headed to the huge shower stall. "Last one in hangs up the towels."

Hank waited until he watched her start the rain shower. He dropped all his clothes there and chuckled. "Everything's going into a laundry basket…. Who cares?" He opened the shower door and cornered Ava amorously.

She squealed as he caught her around the waist and spun her under the water. "You're the one showering, not me."

He let Ava go and then chose the fluffy body puff and soap. "I'd appreciate a little help washing my back."

Ava accepted the tool of her happy trade. "Okay, handsome, turn around and hands flat on the wall."

"But I like to look at you all wet."

"That's coming." She giggled mischievously as she soaped up the body puff.

Hank's knees went a little weak as she worked the puff across his broad shoulders. In the bathroom's mirror, he got all kinds of satisfaction watching her trail the soap bubbles down the center of his back. His back arched as her fingertips danced through the bubbles, encouraging them to spread across the cheeks of his ass.

It struck him that a week ago, being here like this with Ava was a fantasy. Each time they met, she intuitively knew just how to calm him down or get him riled up for all the right reasons. He never expected such romance at this point in his life. It felt damn good.

"Well, turnabout is fair play."

"Ohh, just three more minutes." His back bowed into her caresses.

"Just three more minutes…"

Hank caught the puff from Ava and gently moved her under the water. Tossing the puff aside, Hank's voice deepened. "When I do turnabouts, puffs just get in my way." He slathered shower gel between his hands and began his loving assault.

Ava looked up at him. "I just realized how big you really are."

Hank rested a foot on the shower seat and leaned into his bubble-filled massaging of her shoulders. He gazed into her eyes and came in for a kiss. *Perhaps a little tongue play?* Just as Hank pressed a kiss to Ava's forehead, he felt a commanding grasp below the belt.

"What's on your mind, Sunshine?" Their lips stayed within a breath of each other, and he refused to move out of her grasp.

"I washed your back, can't neglect the front." Her hands worked together on two separate parts of him. Both were relentless in dispensing all sorts of electric pleasure.

His hands flew to the shower wall to endure this amorous onslaught. His words came out on a growl. "Ava, Sunshine, do you know what you're doing to me?"

Ava blew him a kiss. "I do. Hang in there…" That's when Hank steeled himself at the stream of warm water flowing over her bubbly work. "I do mean hang in there." He felt her cup his sac as her lips surrounded his flesh.

"Oh! I wasn't expecting this. I was hoping for it, but…. Ohh, Ava, you little fox." The last of his words came out with a lusty roar.

She looked up at him, wiping the shower water off her face. "I'm sorry. I neglected to ask if that was okay."

Hank dropped next to her on the shower seat and wrapped his arms around her, pulling her onto his lap. Nuzzling into her ear, he whispered. "Beyond okay, Sunshine, that was mind-blowing."

Their wet bodies wrestled as they kissed, leaving Ava straddling his lap. "Yeah, you are mind-blowing. I'm enjoying this shower."

"Next time you'll enjoy it even more because I have some surprises for you." Hank ran his hands sensually down her body.

She kissed him, sealing his promise. "Oh, Hank, this is just so…"

They shared a long gaze. Hank nodded. "Yeah, it's hard to believe all the good things we've enjoyed so far."

The good 'things' continued until they were spent. They staggered to stand and rinsed off each other. Hank got on with the business of looking and dressing like James Bond. Ava laid each piece of his wardrobe on the bed.

Hank strolled out of the bathroom and did a double-take. "Oh, my, do you have any spy stuff for me?"

Ava held open a jewel box. "This is your earpiece. Jax said it's very important to get it in deep.

Hank caught Ava by the waist, bending her back, he affected a British accent. "You know I like it deep." They shared a quick kiss, and he righted her. "I can't call you Moneypenny because she was always frustrated. I can't call you Q because that's too scientific. But I can call you Mmmm."

Ava looked up at him. 'Don't you mean M, who was the big boss?

With a chuckle, he shook his head. "No, I mean mmmm delicious."

She playfully swatted his bare behind with a towel. "I don't think there was a Bond Girl named Delicious. Get dressed."

****

When the Eurocopter landed on The Vesper's helipad, the ship's crew gathered to see this odd-looking flying machine. Before Hank and Kirk disembarked, they caught Peng's curious expression as he noticed the Mele Lani logo and name in red. Hank sniffed as they watched Peng through the window of the bridge. "You think he's writing down the tail number?"

Kirk harrumphed. The men followed their escort directly to Seventh Heaven, where Hank was introduced to the other players and finally, Peng himself.

Peng nodded regally. "I'm honored to have you join us tonight, my friend."

Hank bowed. "The honor is mine, my friend." As Hank stepped back from that introduction, he read the room. His arrival changed the tenor. Now it was a party.

A voluptuous young woman led him toward the buffet table, but he diverted her to his formidable floral arrangement in the corner of the room. *Is everyone watching me?* He plucked one of the bird of paradise blooms from the pot and ran its foliage down his companion's arm. Just loud enough for Peng to hear, he declared.

"This is the way I like my women, colorful and wild." His fingers danced over the trio of orange tepels, moving to the sheltering folded leaf holding the bloom in close examination. Hank verified the tiny transmitter was well hidden, but he also felt the room's scrutiny. He had to squeeze the flower's sheath to activate the transmitter. With a pinch, he heard the low beep in his ear. "Ahh." He stabbed the frond deep within the pot's dirt.

In seconds, Peng was at his elbow. "Do you like it rough?"

Hank shrugged as he turned to Peng. "Who doesn't, my friend?"

Peng laughed as he gestured to the women in the room. "Any one of these ladies will be happy to oblige you." The dark-haired beauty in the cobalt dress was back, and she brought friends.

Hank thought he'd have to fight his way to the poker table. Other players watched covetously as two women book ended Hank as he walked.

With a nod from Peng, the players took their seats. Hank scrubbed his hands together. "Time to play cards."

His right-hand woman whispered in his ear. "Good luck." *Did she just slip me some tongue?* Peng pivoted away to take his seat at the hexagonal table. *Good dog. Sit. Stay. Play.*

Thanks to Jax's bird's-eye view, Hank easily bested most of the table's occupants. He almost always found himself playing the Aussie or Peng for the pot. The Aussie didn't say much, his poker face unreadable. Hank's gaze caught Kirk visibly bristling at wearing formal wear.

Although Jax's hand-by-hand commentary afforded Hank every advantage, the dealer gave Hank plenty to bluff about. *I'm damn lucky Jax knows the game.* A few times, Hank gulped when Jax advised 'raise him ten thousand dollars,' but he managed to do it in General-mode. *Thank God, I learned to bluff in the military.*

Hank observed by the time the first pot sat in front of Peng, the early folders were led away from the table by their fawning escorts. Hank almost jumped when Jax chuckled in his ear. "They're going to get their ashes hauled." Hank dropped his chin and nodded his head.

Peng addressed Hank across the table. "Losing has its consolations at this game, my friend."

Hank watched the Asian lady in her forties leaving on the arm of a fabulously built young man in a slim tux. "So, I've noticed. You have a most attractive stable of companions…"

Peng raised an ironic brow. "Not only attractive, but skilled and accommodating." He nodded toward the bar girl to bring another drink to Hank. "You may wish to take advantage of my hospitable employees yourself."

Hank put a hand over his barely touched bourbon and gave Peng a steely glance. "When I play cards, I keep a clear head and my mind on the game."

Peng settled in his chair and smiled. "A man after my own heart." Hank noticed new players being greeted at the staircase. Peng nodded. "Fresh blood. Shall we raise the stakes?"

The next hand was brutal. Each new card player fell to either Peng or Hank's skill.

****

Running a finger around his stiff collar, Kirk wondered where the 'madam' was. Certainly, there was someone in charge of the sex workers because that's what they were. He recognized the card players' demeaning stares at the companions circling them. Kirk knew he was viewed as hired help, one step above the sex workers. He wasn't fed, he wasn't watered. He was invisible. *Sometimes, invisibility is an asset.*

As the play heated up, Kirk slipped out of Seventh Heaven, following the trail of overwhelming perfume wafting from a middle-aged woman on the arm of her stud. *They're taking them to staterooms. Where are the barracks? Who's the puppet master? Where are the guards?*

That question was answered quickly enough when one of the gorilla twins stepped into his narrow path. Kirk jerked his chin. "Godzilla, which way to the head?"

The mean man narrowed his gaze. "Godzilla?" His voice was an octave higher than Kirk expected.

Kirk played with the guy. He gestured to himself. "You know me, I work for Peng."

The guy gave him a grunting pass. "We all work for Mr. Huang."

Kirk nearly bounced on his feet to get out of this guy's sight. "So, where did all this skin come from?"

The guy tilted his head and then nodded. "Ah, skin, yes."

Kirk held out his hands. "This is a huge boat, but they all can't live here. Where do they come from?"

Godzilla turned surly with a string of words that ended with, "I dunno." He flattened himself against the wall so Kirk could pass. "The head, that way, second door."

Going through the second door, Kirk saw two guards this time. This had to mean he was either getting closer to the barracks or the exit. *Still no mammasan. Maybe I can find out more from Peng later.*

As they had intended, Hank was able to play Peng to a virtual draw. Kirk watched Hank as he out-alphaed Peng when it came to setting boundaries. And when the smiling, middle-aged woman returned for the last hand, before she sat, Hank made a show of slipping her his business card. "You show this card at the door of Mele Lani. Ask for Richard. He'll show you a good time." He winked.

Peng's gaze narrowed as his face flushed red. Kirk smirked as ire melted into jealousy. At the end of the evening, when Hank looked at his watch, Peng caught Kirk by the elbow. "Don't leave. Let him go."

Kirk cocked a brow. "Competition a little too stiff?"

Peng sniffed. "Of course not. He ignored my extraordinary … girls."

Kirk thought about Peng's inability to think of his stable as human. He laughed. "Seriously? His girls are highly trained to his specifications. When you imagine sex and this man? Take it to a whole other level. His appetites won't be satisfied in the time it takes to play a hand of cards. Be happy he expressed an interest in returning."

A storm emerged in Peng's dark eyes as he shot his cuffs and headed to the bar.

****

When Seventh Heaven closed and the ship went dark, Kirk ambled down the gangplank, thumbing his phone for a ride. The marina nightclub still belched out bad karaoke as he ordered a club soda and waited.

Under cover of darkness, a line of men and women were led away. The gorilla twins split, one at the front of the line, one at the back. Kirk sat in awe of such a large group's docile compliance. *Threats against their families' lives? This could be a problem.*

Jax pulled up in an unremarkable car and together they tailed the tourist bus full of sex workers. Kirk gestured. "You got here just in time. As large as that ship is, it couldn't hold all of them."

Jax followed a couple of car lengths back and turned the corner when the bus pulled to a stop at a chain-link gate and honked its horn. An armed guard sauntered to open the locked six-foot entry.

Once Jax and Kirk watched the gate close, they snuck closer. Wildly unkempt foliage covered the surrounding fence topped by two feet of circular razor wire. Jax motioned Kirk over. "You can barely see this place from the street. The Devil Weed has covered the fence." Kirk pinned the location on his phone, and they rode home.

133

****

Ava met Hank at the front door, vibrating with excitement. "Tell me everything." She helped him off with his tuxedo jacket, but Hank held on.

"Wait a minute. Let me clean out the pockets…" Both hands dug deep and retrieved four stacks of cash. "What a night. Have you heard from Kirk yet?"

Chapter Twelve

The following night, Ava carried the freshly pressed tux back to Hank. "Care to have your back washed for good luck?"

Hank dropped his jacket on the bed and hugged Ava tightly. He nuzzled her ear and whispered, "Why not?"

Once Ava marked her man, he dressed and waited for Kirk's call. Before he left, Ava tacked an enamel anthurium pin to his lapel. "Wouldn't it be clever for this to be the identifying pin for your sex club?"

Hank chuckled. "Sunshine, when I leave you to your devices, you get downright crafty. Are you going to crochet any of those little weenie warmers for guests who might catch a cold?

"My craftiness ended here. Now, he'll know you're hung like a stallion."

Hank opened his mouth, stammered, and shut up. His phone rang, it was Kirk.

"Teflon, we're leaving from the dock at the Hilton."

"Dock?"

Kirk chuckled. "We have to show Peng all the toys. Tonight, we have a sleek boat to get us to The Vesper."

****

Bikini-clad tourists stared at the two men in tuxedos walking the jetty's length to a sleek 1920s Italian-built Vapporeto Runabout. Hiatt's renovation of the boat included a stealth makeover. From the gleaming black hull to the ebony leather seating, to the red logo for Mele Lani, this boat was made to be gossiped about.

Hank shot his cuffs as he turned and nodded generically to the looky-loos. "Kirk, my life has been a lot more exciting since I retired."

Kirk took a seat. "Wait till they catch the name when we pull away."

One couple waiting for the booze cruise laughed when the boat turned and took off. *The Domme* sped toward *The Vesper*.

****

Once Kirk called Peng and requested the lower bay opened for their arrival, it was no surprise they were a spectacle. Most of the players hung over the side of The Vesper to watch Kirk and the General arrive. When the runabout turned and disappeared, it was back to boozing and gossip.

As Hank assumed his gambler persona, Kirk hung back. He watched Peng observe as some of last night's players greeted the General effusively.

An elderly Indonesian, Candra Bulan, was the only person ignoring the ruckus over Hank's arrival. With a meaningful glance in Kirk's direction, Hank sought the ninety-year-old man who was a regular at Seventh Heaven. Hank delivered the sembah greeting which closely resembled 'namaste.' With a respectful tone, he bowed and practically shouted at the moderately deaf man. "I'm honored to play with you again, Pak. I have learned watching your skill."

The aged Bulan's smile creased his happy eyes and in Kirk's estimation, Hank was the venerated codger's new best friend. As the social hour concluded, Hank managed to interact with every player except Peng. Now was the time for Hank to pull Peng aside before they ascended the steps to Seventh Heaven. Once Kirk saw their heads together in the corner, he had to squelch his grin. Being Peng's man on the floor, Kirk stood, shielding them from the other's view.

Hank put a tone of genuine concern in his words. "May I offer you some words of advice as a man who has dealt professionally with the public for many years?" Kirk fought the smile from his face as he heard Peng's grunt in response. "You keep people at a distance. How can you get your hands in their pockets if you don't hold them closer?"

Kirk closed his eyes tightly, waiting for a bomb to go off.

Peng sucked air between his teeth. "You came in tonight and spoke with everyone but me."

Hank scoffed. "I was sure you'd be outraged after I beat you last night."

Kirk could imagine the astonishment in Peng's eyes. "It wasn't the lack of the win. It was the lack of an invitation, though I saw you invite Madam Xue to your resort."

Hank's voice became patronizing. "Madam Xue was recommended to me by one of my dearest friends. Do you know Ronnie Tengfeng? I have to rely on my members' approvals to keep my standards."

Kirk's self-restraint evaporated, and he turned to watch Peng's reply. He couldn't miss the two red flags of irritation burning in the man's cheeks.

"As it happens, I went to school with Syaoran. We've known each other all our lives." Peng shot Kirk an icy stare and Kirk shrugged.

Hank's face brightened. "Then you should ask Ronnie to sponsor you. In fact, I was stunned he's not here. You must know how he loves poker. I'll consult with him." Hank waved Kirk over. "While we're playing, call Mele Lani and see if Ronnie is free." He turned back to Peng. "You may have your invitation by our first break."

Pulling away from Hank, Peng glared at Kirk, who found himself neatly cornered. "I know you heard that." Peng lowered his voice to a hiss. "What have I been paying you for?"

Kirk puffed up his chest and stood taller than Peng. "If it weren't for me, you wouldn't occupy the same airspace as the General." Peng sniffed. "The General is your key to Ronnie." Kirk gestured skyward.

Peng straightened his tie and backed away from Kirk, his hospitality returning. "Friends, our games await." He gestured his guests forward and observed Hank flirting with the two companions who flanked him.

Both Hank's arms curled around the women's waists. "Ladies, do you know the sensation of a well-delivered spanking?" The ladies shared a wide-eyed glance before they covered their mouths to giggle. "Well, of course, you don't, because I haven't paddled you… yet."

Hank made it seem as if he had a streak of colossally bad luck. In truth, his cards were excellent, but at Jax's instruction, he looked appropriately morose. Hank brightened only when hearing Kirk's overly loud announcement, "General, Tengfeng wants to speak to you personally."

Hank folded his hand, tipped the dealer, and turned to Peng. "Excuse me for a moment, won't you?"

****

By the time Hank returned to the table, Peng called the first break of the evening and beelined to him like a junior high gossip. Hank thought, *I believe I have his balls in my pocket.*

Peng wasted no time. "Well?"

Hank took a step back from the man. "It happens that Ronnie confirmed that you *were* schoolmates. He did say he wasn't sure you were the caliber of player we wanted." Hank shoved his hands in his pockets. "I tried to reassure him that you could hold your own in every situation. But Ronnie was not so sure. He suggested he play here tomorrow night to make his decision."

Through gritted teeth, Peng whispered. "Are you not your own man?"

Hank gave him a wry smile. "I am, and Ronnie Tengfeng is my chief investor. If you want to play the game on a grand scale, you too will have to learn to work with investors. You'll prove yourself soon enough… I think your companions could be ripe for an introduction to my entertainment style."

Peng's head swiveled to stare at him. "Are you proposing paying me for my stable? This could be beneficial for both of us."

Hank bowed his head. "Variety is the very spice that gives life its flavor." He turned away and stepped back. "Let's go play cards."

Hank did not miss the look of calculation in Peng's eyes, nor the elation when Hank repeatedly folded or played worthless hands. All in all, the night was a success. Kirk and Hank could see the anticipation mounting in Peng's effusive farewells. Tonight, Kirk took his leave before Hank boarded the runabout.

****

To confirm the living arrangements of The Vesper's companions, Jax and Kirk followed the white tour bus to the ramshackle motor court. This time, Jax skirted the long wall of weed-covered chain-link fence to snap photos from the hillside above.

Back in the car, Jax shook his head. "Did you see that outdoor kitchen?"

Kirk chuckled. "I'm your old man and I sit in the car. What kind of kitchen?"

"The old place is so run down; they cook under a tarp. There's nothing but cauldrons and noodles drying overnight."

****

Ava cursed the ringing phone. Light seeped through the blackout curtains as she squinted over Hank to check the clock. Without looking at the caller ID, she answered. "Hello?"

"Ava, doll, where are you?" It was Victor.

Ava sat up in bed as Hank snuffled and rolled on his back, still asleep. "Where am I? Where are you at this time of the morning?"

"I just ordered the most extravagant mimosa and told them to put your name on it."

Ava heard voices and Muzak in the background. "All kidding aside, Victor? Where are you?"

"I took your advice. I've come to find myself in Hawaii…"

Ava ran a hand through her hair. "Find your… self. Where are you finding yourself?"

"I'm at the Royal Hawaiian. I've booked one of those snazzy historic ocean suites."

She watched sleeping Hank's jaw drop, and the snoring began. She jumped out of bed and scurried to the living room. "That's nice. Here on a convention?"

"I thought I'd take a trip to kill a little time."

"Unh, huh?"

"So, come over and claim your mimosa. What, you live a couple of blocks from here?"

She bit her top lip. "When did we last talk?" She put down the phone and turned on the speaker while she made coffee. *I really need coffee.*

"The day you landed after the sale."

"You know what I said about being free?"

His voice became cautious. "Yes, that was my reason for the trip…"

"Did they declare Sheldon dead?"

"I brought you the papers myself. Thought this might be the start of something good."

She bit harder on her lip and closed her eyes. This thing with Hank was moving from warm to hot at warp speed. She had not discussed Sheldon's true 'status'. She picked up the phone and turned off the speaker. With a deep breath, she sighed. "Something good? I'm always open to a friend bearing gifts." She turned to stare out of the dining-room window. The beat of silence between them grew awkward. Ava's voice softened. "On the flight home, I met an incredible man…"

Victor harrumphed. "You work fast."

"That's the wonderful thing. It wasn't work at all. We clicked before we even spoke. I hope you haven't come here for me…" Blood roared in Ava's ears. These past few days, neither Hank nor Ava labeled what blossomed between them.

"Well, to be honest, Ava, I kind of did. You know, the two of us were always stuck in the corner at parties while our spouses held the limelight. I sort of saw us like old friends who could grow to be more."

Ava shook her head and pressed her wrist against her forehead. "I will always be your friend and I so appreciate everything you've done for me…" There was silence on the line as she pushed him into the 'friend zone'. She wished he would say something. *Am I nuts with what I'm about to say?* "Victor, I'm in love. He's everything exciting about life, his family is welcoming and genuine. He's what I want in a man."

Victor sighed. "Am I hearing a marvelous fairy tale?"

Ava caught a tiny tear of happiness. "You know, Victor, gals like me need to be romanced. For some people, friendship is enough, but not for me. I need bottle rockets and jet planes."

"Well, babe, I'll leave the papers for you at the front desk." He chuckled. "I made reservations for some great island excursions. I think I need to scout out Miss Right Now."

When Ava closed the call, she turned to see Hank leaning against the bedroom doorjamb. "How much did you hear?"

"Enough to know I have some competition." He gestured expansively. "Of course, I should have anticipated that."

Ava wiped away that silly tear and covered her mouth with her hand for fear of what might fly out. Her gaze fell on the kitchen, and she plastered on a bright smile. *The ball is in his court.* "How would you like your eggs?"

****

Hank needed more than a three-minute egg to process what he'd overheard. "Did you know I make the best pineapple pancakes with guava syrup?"

"I did not, but it sounds great. Do I have time for a shower?"

Hank caught her around the waist, planted a kiss on her forehead, and spun her in the direction of the bathroom. "Sure." He watched her skitter away, turned, and considered what he'd heard. *Do I need to make a decision here?* He fell back on his scientific schooling. *Are we romantic fission or fusion? Fusion is unbridled and costly to create. How much heart have I invested in her? Did I just hear her reject a proposal in favor of me? Am I willing to ante up?*

Ava arrived on a cloud of that irresistible smoky cologne of hers while he beat pancake batter into submission with just a wire whisk.

"Did it attack you? You're making that batter pay."

Hank stood in his boxers with the large bowl under his arm, the whisk dripping back into the bowl. "You gotta show pineapple who's boss." He turned and put down the bowl, running his hand through his hair. "What's on your agenda today?" He looked down at his lack of clothing. "Hold that thought. I'll be right back."

As Hank threw on cargo shorts and a shirt, he heard the chairs move and silverware being placed. She was setting up the dining room. *That's a serious place to eat. We've always eaten on the lanai. Oh, God...*

****

Between Hank, Kirk, and Ronnie, they had enough close-quarters training to handle anything Peng might throw at them, but Ronnie's three extra bodyguards were impressive. *Perception is reality.*

As the runabout flew across the waves, Hank caught Ronnie's broad grin. He and Kirk weren't the only ones enjoying their caper.

****

As expected, everyone aboard The Vesper, having heard a special guest boarded tonight, turned to watch them alight from the long black boat. Tonight, Peng waited for them amid the water toys in the garage. Peng extended a hand. "Ronnie, hao jiu bu jian?

Of course, you haven't seen me in a while, motherfucker. Ronnie grew a cultured smile and replied "Nínhǎo."

Peng's smile evaporated at the basic hello, but he seemed to gather himself and gestured expansively toward the stairs. Hank spoke up. "Thank you for greeting us personally." Hank stood back and let the new guest follow Peng.

"Welcome to my superyacht." Ronnie looked around feigning disinterest, declining comment. "It is a pearl of the South Pacific, where it was made three years ago to my specifications."

Ronnie dropped his chin. *Pearl? Like earrings, do you have two?* He wiped that smile off his face and replied by moving his hand from the top of his gleaming black hair to the pristine white overhead. "Are the upper decks more spacious?"

As Peng turned to go up the next set of steps, his smile straightened. "Yes, all public areas are ten feet high." As they ascended the stairs, the music and laughter grew louder.

143

Hank leaned in toward Ronnie. "Wait till you see the bar, some of the finest whiskeys in the world."

That brought a grin to Ronnie's face and Peng enthused. "You'll find our games second to none."

Ronnie nodded to Hank. "My friend, the General, assures me you've developed hospitality and skills since our school days."

Peng gestured to the women around the piano, urging them to greet his guests. "Boys grow into men and my companions are here to meet your every need." Peng situated himself among the twelve companions and smiled proudly. "As my guest, please choose your companions, Ronnie. Please choose as many you like."

Standing with his hands clasped in front of him, Ronnie considered the group. "My friend, I am amazed at their reserved dress. They look…" He searched for the word. "Bland. I thought you would be offering more titillation, but then I'm undoubtedly spoiled by my experiences at Mele Lani."

Peng's expression turned envious. "I can only offer what I know, as I have never been invited to Mele Lani."

Ronnie wanted to turn the screws a little tighter, but right now, it was better to feint at taking Peng's money. "I know what we are all here for." He regarded the other players grabbing a last drink as they settled in their seats. Although Ronnie counted cards successfully, he wore an earpiece like Hank's, so they were on the same wavelength. To confirm tonight's strategy, Ronnie grinned at Hank. "General, are we letting our host win this one?" Both men heard Jax's laughter and positive response.

****

Hank drew considerable enjoyment from watching the 'Peng and Ronnie' show. The rest of the table needn't have shown up tonight. Competent players fell away like dried flowers, leaving their chips in heaps. Hank kept his gaze locked on his hand as Ronnie conversationally taunted Peng. "My friend, do you like watersports?"

Peng sat up straighter and smiled. "My entire garage below holds everything for enjoying this beautiful ocean."

The old guy from San Francisco couldn't restrain his laughter. "Excuse me, bahahaha, where I come from, that's not watersports." He couldn't restrain his thoughts.

Ronnie raised half a grin and nodded. "Allow me to invite you to our club. Have you heard of Mele Lani? You're the sort of fellow who fits right in."

The older gentleman looked down at his cards and demurred. "I didn't say it was my kink, but I know it doesn't involve jet skis."

Ronnie chuckled. "Just so, but we have a cafeteria of kink. I'm sure we'll have something to your liking.

Ronnie's head snapped up at Peng's abrupt words. "Why not me? Why am I not invited?" He slapped his cards on the felt and looked around. Speaking to Hank, Peng's words hissed out. "You did this to me and now he's here inviting everyone but me."

Hank deferred to Ronnie. The two men nodded, and Ronnie spoke. "Why don't we let lady luck decide?" He regarded the pot and the fact that half the table had folded.

"Meaning?" Peng was resentful.

"Meaning we can draw cards for the opportunity. If you win, you come to the club. But you pay me the pot. If I win, I take the pot and leave."

Peng's brows knit. "You win either way."

Ronnie shrugged. "In the words of Browning, 'ah, but a man's reach should exceed his grasp, or what's a heaven for?'" That met with chilly silence, so Ronnie plunged on with a flourish. "Is this not Seventh Heaven? Do you not enjoy these carnal pleasures? From the looks on the faces of the returning players, they're satisfied."

The gauntlet was thrown, and players pushed back an inch or so to extract themselves from the coming storm.

Peng's fury exploded from his entire being. "My companions can stand shoulder to shoulder with any you may have."

Ronnie smiled with a slow nod. "Then, draw your card."

Peng turned over the king of hearts, but Ronnie turned over the ace of diamonds. There was a gasp from the crowd. Peng's eyes flamed. "Double or nothing."

Ronnie gave him a long, searching stare. "I'm moved by your need. Double or nothing. However, this time, if you win, you become a member of Mele Lani with all the privileges that entails. If I win, you may visit, but you bring your entire stable with you and we play truth or dare." Ronnie tapped his index finger on the felt. "Every one of your companions, no leaving your favorites at home."

Peng's eyes were fever bright. His knuckles rapped on the felt. "Agreed."

Jax's voice went dry in Ronnie's ear. "Ten-Fingers, let's hope you're the player I remember."

Ronnie chuckled and Peng's head inclined like the dog before the gramophone. "Dealer, let's play cards."

****

As far as Hank was concerned, this was the game that crawled like honey in January. When the round of betting finished, there were three shared cards dealt face up in the middle of the table. Staring back at Hank were a three of spades, a five of hearts, and a jack of diamonds.

Hank watched Ronnie's poker face. *Damn, the man is impenetrable.* The rest of the table sat fascinated; their own wallets emptied into the pot. At the turn, the dealer revealed a queen of diamonds.

Peng's gaze swept the table as he paused. "I raise you five hundred thousand." He moved his chips into the pot.

Ronnie's brow rose in acceptance. "I see your five hundred thousand and raise you two hundred and fifty thousand."

The dealer revealed the fifth and final card, the four of spades. "Gentlemen?"

Smirking, Peng nodded. "Five hundred thousand."

Jax snickered into Hank's ear. "Wait for it." Hank sniffed. Kirk ran a finger inside his stiff shirt collar. The air conditioner kicked in and the feathers in the Asian woman's comb fluttered.

Ronnie sat forward and moved his chips. "All in."

Hank sipped his drink, mentally counted the bounty in the pot, and chewed the end of his unlit pipe while listening to Jax.

Hank heard Jax whisper. "Ronnie, Peng is about to lose his shit, just like I did the last time you and I played."

Peng sat proudly and uncovered two queens, plus the queen in the community cards. "Three lovely and willing ladies."

Hank could see tractor beams psychically moving the pot in Peng's direction until Ronnie exposed his cards. "My two of spades and a six of diamonds make a nice straight with those," he nodded to the community cards, the three of spades, the five of hearts, and the four of spades.

The players at the table vibrated with amazement. The dealer nodded to Ronnie. "Mr. Tengfeng wins with a straight."

With a casual air, Ronnie wrapped his arms around the multi-million-dollar pot and brought it toward him.

Peng was half out of his chair. "Double or nothing, *again...*"

Ronnie gave him a look of reprimand. "I cannot oblige you; I have a date." He stacked the chips to cash them in. He rose and bowed from the shoulders. "What a pleasure this has been with all of you."

"You must allow me a rematch," Peng insisted.

Ronnie looked him up and down. "You agreed if I win, you may visit, but you bring your entire stable with you. I may agree to a rematch in the future. Wasn't the point of this game to win an invitation to Mele Lani?"

Stammering in the faces of the building crowd, Peng spat out. "Yes, but you have my money and when I visit, you will also enjoy my companions. This was winner take all."

Ronnie paused a considering beat and leaned forward, his palms on the table, looking up at Hank. "What did I tell you? He's a poor loser. He gains his desired entry to Mele Lani and whines about losing money. He is a child."

At those words, Kirk and the gorilla twins stood by Peng in a show of force. Peng's tone cut the air. "Very well. I will be at your resort at nine in the evening. I'll need the coordinates."

Hank shook his head. "My friend, we will have our pilot arrive tomorrow by eight for The Vesper's sailing to the resort. That's our policy. There will be a tally of your companions. Don't hold out on us."

Peng stood chastened. "Then I will be ready."

****

After the men left, there was still sun in the sky and inviting waves on the beach. Ava jotted a note on a large piece of paper and secured it with a heavy mug on Hank's bedside table.

> *Handsome,*
>
> *I hope the night went perfectly. Victor left me legal papers at the Royal Hawaiian's front desk. I'm picking them up and then going over to my place.*
>
> *My condo needs a little fresh air. I'll be spending the night there. Call me in the morning.*
>
> *XO XO, Sunshine*

Chapter Thirteen

Ava dressed for herself tonight and spritzed on her floral cologne to blend with the tropical gardens at the resort. Once she drank a fruity Mai Tai and ate a tray of vegetable spring rolls, she checked her watch, hoping to avoid Victor in the hotel lobby. From what he said about the excursions, she would miss Victor and Ms. Right Now by a couple of hours.

Dangling her sandals on her fingertips, she made a slow trip toward the Royal Hawaiian front desk. *Of course, when I'm trying to blend in, every hotel staff member greets me. Especially the one I have trouble finding when I have an event.*

It took her several minutes to look at two different sets of grandbaby pictures. When she got to the front desk, she whispered, "Victor Barry left an envelope for Ava Hansen, please."

The evening manager's eyes brightened at her voice. "I was hoping you would be our guest with Mr. Barry. I owe you so much. I wanted to treat the two of you to something extra." He slid the thick envelope across the counter, and she mentally rolled her eyes and waved him off.

"Mako, you are the soul of hospitality. Maybe another time."

She held the envelope to her chest and, exiting the front door, realized it had grown dark. Just for safety's sake, she hailed a cab home.

****

Her condo was stuffy, even with the air conditioning. She walked through, seeing her wilted plants. *I have to fire the maid. Oh, wait, I am the maid. I better water the plants.* She dropped the envelope on the desk and opened all the windows to enjoy the cleansing night breeze.

She was surrounded by her favorite fragrances and the comfort of her specially selected belongings. *I am home.*

Peng isn't thinking about me. He's too busy playing cards and sucking up to an invitation to Mele Lani. She sat barefooted and ran her toes back and forth on her velvety carpet. *Am I sick of tile floors yet?* The bra came off, flying through the sleeve of her muumuu. She got out the blender and made an adult drink from frozen fruit and rum. *I don't trust one piece of fruit in that bowl.* She dumped the bowl's contents into the garbage. Dialing up soft music, she carried the entire blender and a fancy glass to her bedroom. She sat at the desk in the corner and drew in a deep breath. Looking out her window, Ava could see Hank's condo. She was glad she left the lights on for him.

With a graceful slice of her mother-of-pearl letter opener, her passport to freedom fell to the table. Her hands on each side of the cover sheet, she gaped at the stack of papers. Pastel post-its noted specific pages Victor thought were important. *Finally, this is here.* She kissed two fingers and sent the kisses airborne. "Sheldon, wherever you are, please stay there."

Ava sipped through a wide straw and recalled their honeymoon as the ship sailed out of San Francisco. Looking at her glass, she reminisced about two young college graduates tasting their first hint of luxury. Sheldon presented her with a five-thousand-dollar windfall from a stock transaction. Otherwise, they would have honeymooned in Fresno. Being a communication major, she didn't know how he did it, and at the time, she didn't care. The workings of the stock market were an ancient financial secret to her.

Everyone thought of Stanford as an elite university, and it was. But she and Sheldon were on scholarship and even at Stanford, dorms were dorms. As newlyweds, they planned for an efficiency apartment in a seamy neighborhood within walking distance of Sheldon's entry-level position at the investment bank.

Why was he on foot? She raised her glass and stared at the lights along the Ala Moana Canal. She shook her head. *I should have had a clue when he sold his car 'because it's more expensive to fix than it's worth.' Then why did I see the poorest kid in your dorm driving that car the next week? Damn gambling debts.*

She flipped pages, glancing at the legalese as she recalled every one of Sheldon's triumphs was veiled larceny.

The frozen concoction of fruit and dark rum had her wheels spinning. Now she was hungry. Throwing open cabinet doors and not finding anything appealing, she sought her stash of Stouffer's frozen dinners. It was nine o'clock and this turkey tetrazzini was going right to her hips. In the six and half minutes it rode the microwave carousel, she decided she didn't care if Sheldon was dead. *He is gone.*

Carrying the black, plastic tray on a hot pad, she returned to her desk and begrudged Sheldon every one of the last five years. At the same time, she applauded herself for struggling through hell with no family help.

Pushing tiny cubes of suspicious turkey back and forth, she grinned at the last page of the paperwork. The life insurance form with Sheldon's bombastic signature showed he had no idea what he was signing the day she pushed a stack of papers in front of him. She smirked. "Thank you, Johnny Walker Blue Label."

He just considered the brief visit from a pretty nurse as a precursor to his next job. The long-awaited life insurance check was artistic with its ornate green curlicue background. The best part was *pay to the order of* Ava Hansen, nine hundred thousand dollars. That would buy three more cake projector sets and a lifetime of security. When she finished the bland frozen dinner, she downed the last of her drink and felt her dread vanquished. She no longer lived under the threat of prison as a person of interest in Sheldon's disappearance.

Now she rested her head on her forearms and listened to the island music coming from random open condo sliding doors. The music danced along with the night breeze. Life is good. *Now I can afford that tee shirt.*

****

Hank laid on what he now considered his side of the bed. The bed seemed like a vast desert of loneliness without Ava. *What was yesterday's early morning phone call about?* Not that she was a player, but she had been free and in circulation longer than he had. *Does she even want a permanent relationship? I mean, she turned down a guy she's known for ages. She did sound pretty positive about me. We've had fireworks. I have a jet plane, in the company's name.*

Hank fisted the sheets and not in that pleasurable, pre-orgasmic way. *Do folks our age go steady? Is it too soon to ask her to commit? Should I give her a promise ring? If I had my way, I'd marry her tomorrow.*

I made a commitment when the whole famn-damily picked up her cause and ran with it. We're risking life and limb with a human trafficker. Does that make me her knight in shining armor? It is amazing how when the need arises, Kirk and Jax are ready for a mission. They need hobbies.

****

As Ava made coffee in her galley kitchen, the check on the desk burned a hole in her mental pocket. Didn't she want a nicer kitchen? *Hank has a gourmet kitchen.* Didn't she want a jacuzzi in her bathroom? *Hank's tub fits us both with room to play… Do I want Hank or his things? I like his things, but I think… I love Hank.*

She shivered and wrapped her arms around herself. *With my money, we could travel, go anywhere we want.* She closed her eyes and envisioned them in Paris or Rome. *Would he freak out if he heard me thinking like this? Well, I've sort of known him for almost a year, corresponding back and forth via emails about his daughter's wedding.*

Earlier that morning, when she sat up in bed, she caught her expression of pure joy. *This is what he does to me, just thinking of him.* She shook her head. *Do I do this to him?*

Ava stared at her condo. While the walls were the latest color and her furniture was carefully gleaned from high-end resale shops, it might as well have been a model home. Everything was perfect, except the plants. They lacked as much attention as they had before she met Hank. Willing the phone to ring, she carried her cell in her robe pocket and at nine o'clock, it rang.

Before she could answer, Hank blurted out, "I miss you. When are you coming ho… I mean to my place?"

He almost asked me when I was coming home. I heard it. She let out a gust of breath. "I coming and I'm bringing my children with me." She looked down at her bedclothes.

"Children? Do you have cats? You know it's not wise on the twenty-fifth floor."

Ava chuckled. "My plants, they miss me. I noticed you don't have any…"

"After years in a wasteland, I have a black thumb. Bring 'em around at your own risk." He snickered and then added. "When will you be here?"

****

Ava arrived with an expanding cart full of lush tropical plants in plastic pots hidden in wicker and rattan baskets.

Hank threw open the door before she knocked and caught her around the waist in a hug. "Sunshine, where have you been all my life?"

She blinked back at him and then to her plants. "Boys and girls, meet your new daddy."

153

Hank shook his head. "They don't get allowances. The first time that bird of paradise doesn't bloom, it's going on the balcony."

As Hank pulled the wagon past her, she rethought the interior lighting. "Some of them might like that." Hank immediately started placing plants where they looked best without regard to the plant's needs. "And this is why you are a serial plant murderer." She followed him, moving plants to their best location. "Just move the furniture around them."

He scratched his head. "It's always been that easy?"

Ava nodded and grinned as she carried a plant to the bedroom. "This one knows how to keep secrets; she knows all of mine."

Hank took the parlor palm and gave it a suspicious look. "She does? She and I need to have a talk when you're in the shower."

Ava winked. "Then I'll be sure the two of us shower together."

"You and me, or you and the plant?"

Ava grinned. "I missed you, too. I say we do things in this bed that will make her blush."

Hank swept her up and bounced her onto the center of the bed. "No time like the present…" He began unbuttoning his shirt, his launch sequence growing evident in his linen shorts.

Laying back, propped up on her elbows, Ava winced. She had to tell him the full story of Sheldon. *Why did I say he deserted me? That probably left Hank wondering about a few details. At any time, did I misrepresent myself? I don't think so…*

Her expression halted Hank's hand at his belt. "Let's get a cup of coffee and talk."

He stood shirtless, his ardor flagging at her comment. "Coffee? Talk? What have I missed?"

Ava skittered down the bed to him and held out her arms. "Handsome, you haven't missed a thing. I need to fill in some blanks."

He sat next to her, picked up his shirt, and softly grunted. "Blanks, huh?"

As he re-buttoned two or three shirt buttons, she bit her lip and stood. "Coffee first. Why don't we have some of that wonderful Kona coffee you have…?"

They took opposite ends of the counter while they stood listening to the drip and spurt of the coffee maker. Hank's head hung down, watching her bring out cups and spoons. "So, what's the deal, Ava?"

She bit her top lip, pulled out the carafe, and poured his cup first. "Biscotti?"

He shot her a side glance. "Information."

She waited for more coffee to brew and poured her a cup, cradling it like a security blanket. "That first night on your lanai," she nodded outside, "I told you I was deserted…"

Hank interrupted. "Did you kill him and bury him in the basement?"

Ava winced. "I was sort of accused of that, but no." She leaned across from him in the kitchen and a gentle smile returned. "To this day, I do not know what happened to him. Although if I were to guess, I'd say he's living in some country without extradition, enjoying other people's money."

Hank's eyes widened. "You're not talking about Sheldon Carmichael, are you?"

"Yes."

His jaw dropped. "I heard about him in the middle of the desert. *They* said his wife was in on the con."

Aghast, Ava looked up at him. "*They* were wrong. If I was in on the con, do you think I'd be *working* in Hawaii? I'd be off somewhere they couldn't find me." She felt his scrutiny. "Our marriage was another traditional thing Sheldon discarded decades ago. I was window dressing. I knew nothing about his business. My point today is that I have been cleared of all suspicion related to his antics. I've been liberated. Sheldon was declared legally dead last week, and I'm now a free woman."

****

Facts were facts. Hank had fallen in love with a married woman. He let out his held breath and his shoulders dropped from tension's release. "Sky's mother and I were very much in love, and we never kept secrets from each other." He frowned and rubbed his forehead. "But in the service, I knew guys who lived whole separate lives their wives knew nothing about."

Ava nodded. "I should have divorced him twenty years ago. But he claimed we were a monument to his success. I led charities and made good things happen. I thought we made the world a better place. If we barely saw each other except for show, that was okay." She suddenly looked uncomfortable at that declaration.

"You deserved better. I wish I had met you sooner. I could have loved you longer…" Their gazes met at his honesty. "So, what ultimately happened?"

Ava shook her head. "I didn't even know he was missing until the FBI knocked on my door at two AM with a search warrant. They tore up the house, told me to get dressed, and dragged me downtown for interrogation. Luckily, my attorney was worth every dime of his charges. I was released and went home to find out Sheldon cleaned out all of our bank accounts twenty-four hours before they knocked."

Hank ran a hand over his mouth and jaw. "Jezuss…"

"I was used to being a kept woman without a job. I'd been putting aside cash since I suspected he had gambling debts. The Feds froze everything, but they didn't know about my bus station locker."

Hank's brows rose. "Do any bus patrons ever use those things?"

"I don't know, housewives with a bankroll do." She cocked her head comically. "You know all those friends of ours? They were ripped off and didn't want any part of me. I was painted with the same brush as Sheldon."

Hank drew in a deep breath. "It wasn't right of them, but once burned, twice shy."

"I was on the sidewalk and needed a job. I thought I had thousands saved in that tote bag in the locker. When I counted it, I had thirty-five hundred dollars in twenty-dollar bills. I dropped Carmichael from my name…"

Hank mused. "Carmichael sounds like a carbuncle."

"…and about as painful." She grinned and continued. "Housing was cheap in Vegas, but setting up an efficiency took every dime. I knew about charity events, so I dyed my hair blonde and got a job as a catering server. I always knew the Feds were watching. That day at the airport, I thought you were one of them."

Hank scoffed and pointed to himself. "Me?"

She shrugged. "My only friend was my attorney, Vincent."

Hank rubbed a thumb over his bottom lip. "The man on the phone the other morning?"

"Yeah. After a year or two, he believed me since Sheldon hadn't ripped him off. He staked me when I bid on providing food and beverages on a golf course."

Hank nodded. "That's how your business started?"

"Yup. I lived and breathed golf events. One of the golfers was the producer for *Escape to Hawaii* and he offered me a job to cater the show. Here I am."

"And no one ever found Sheldon?"

Ava groaned. "It's not like they weren't looking for him. When you're infamous, even the mob looks for you."

"So, what do you think?" Hank topped off their coffees.

"What I know is more important. He's declared dead. His life insurance policy paid out, and I'm a free woman."

Hank was silent for a long beat. "I don't imagine you're anxious to jump into another… relationship."

"It's amazing how a woman wears that armor for protection. I've put men under microscopes when they've come calling. But there you were, everywhere I turned… You're relentless, Hank. And no, I'm not at all hesitant about you." She paused and stared him down. "Unless my confession has turned you off."

"Turned me off? Hell, Ava, it just shows me what you're made of. You've got moxie and I like moxie."

Her brow arched. "Moxie, huh?"

"Whatever it is, from the day I watched you ride that baggage carousel, I've thought, that's the gal for me." He inclined his head. "Did you really buy almost three grand of shoes?"

She developed a shyer persona. "I'm wearing the flats right now."

They both stared at the crystal-covered gold flat. "Aren't you a little overdressed for a confession?"

She put her cup down and stepped toward him. "We're both overdressed. Let's make that plant blush.

Hank turned it on. He knew women never got enough of the right strokes. It was great fun to strike the right balance with his tongue: No tongue at all felt like junior high, too much tongue felt like honeymoon sex. What's the right amount? If he had to ask, he wasn't doing it right. He knew Ava was aching to get down to business. He also knew delayed pleasure was the best pleasure.

With a firm hand, Hank grasped the hair at the nape of Ava's neck. He drew her slowly to his lips as her blue eyes widened in anticipation. He held her tightly as he nibbled her bottom lip. Being close, feeling her arms reflexively tightening around his torso, he moaned against her. The vibration shuddered through her and kept his erection bobbling. Her lips responded with the sweetest pucker. She suckled back, and they smiled into each other's kiss.

"Mmm, aren't you tasty?"

"Tasty? I'm glad… My goddess, it's all about unblocking our bliss." He knew that look. Ava's vibrant expression darkened to sexual hunger. His lips moved to the shell of her ear and, still holding her in place, his open mouth skated the curve, and he inhaled.

"Ahhh." She let out a deep gasp.

Almost biting her earlobe, he chuckled. "I could dine on you forever. Ava, let's get lost in our desire." His teeth caught her earlobe, and he gently tugged. "You know, I can do this to other parts of you, too." She swayed into him, and he laid her back on the bed. His fingertips walked down her cleavage, tickling, and teasing her tight flesh. "I've been thinking about doing things to you all day, but now I seem to be stuck on just doing this." His palm covered her nest of dusky hair at her delta. With a gentle nip on her neck, his fingers stroked her anxious flesh. She bowed into his touch with a moan. Hank upped the ante, bit, and released her neck without leaving a mark. They shuddered together, him enjoying her responses.

His lips left her flesh to ask. "Do you know the rule of the nipple?" She shyly shook her head. "Nipples are the key to everything. I've watched your nipples since we came in the door tonight. They asked me if I like kissing them. Did you get my psychic message?"

Ava's eyelids fluttered. "Who knew?"

His mouth devoured her taut, rosy peak as his thumb played lightly on her sex. "You are so beautiful like this" His tongue flicked at the rise he excited. "I'd like you to do this to me." He placed her hand on his chest and rolled to his back, still stroking her, bringing her along.

"You do? Ohh…"

"Sunshine, anything you do with those lips would please me… but let's not get ahead of ourselves."

Her hand ran to his sac as her lips sought his nipple. These sensations released a torrent of need.

Moaning against her breasts, his words came out low and slow. "Do you know how good that feels?"

Ava laughed gently against him and fell onto his broad, muscled chest. "Unh, huh?" Her lips never stopped their assault.

Hank sought her soft and magical gaze. "I need you, Ava, being here, like this is my fountain of youth." He smoothed back her wild tendrils of hair and held her forehead to his. He could smell her on his fingers, and before he pressed her back to the pillow, he licked them with a shiver. "You taste delicious." While her eyes widened at his declaration, he flipped over her to straddle him.

****

Together, they anticipated each other's moves. They responded with surprising joy, raw joy, soulful joy, bodily joy. Each move became their horizontal ballet. This loving, old soldier was her perfect partner in seeking and finding this deeply tuned affection. His mastery of her body stirred anarchy within her. With every stroke, they met in a poignant communion.

She rode the waves of his thrusts and parry, meeting him, challenging him to ride harder. With her strong legs straddling him, her back arched, eyes closed, his chest covered with their mingled sweat, and sweet anarchy overcame them.

She'd never experienced physical chaos unexplainable by words, simply uttered in breaths and moans. Her first full breath carried her release. A release that flung her into becoming his. Hank Kingston was everything she wanted. He was everything she never knew she needed. That first time felt like luck. This time felt like forever. With the last gasp of their completion, they took their first breath of being 'them.'

****

Hank held her in one arm as they came back to earth. He caressed Ava's arms in long, light strokes. "Do I make you happy, here, like this?" It was the hard question he had never asked a woman. In his newly widowed, wilding nights, he never cared. But that was a couple of decades ago and he regretted those nights.

Ava curled her legs up and swung one over his body. At first, she covered her smiling face and drew in a deep breath. "Happy, as in, you make me come?"

Hank looked to the ceiling for a beat and nodded, switching his strokes down her thigh laying over him. "That's part of it." He turned more on his side. "I hoped I touched more than that. I know you have sleeping demons from the way you talked about the past."

Ava nodded in realization, and she caught his hand and held it over her heart. "I saw someone the other day. They hadn't seen me in six months. She asked me what my secret was… makeup? Diet?" She placed their hands over Hank's heart. "I simply told her I found love. I didn't need tell her it was the kind of love that wrapped itself around me long after we leave this bed."

Hank clutched her to his chest. They gently rolled in a slow rhythm that matched their heartbeats. "Then would you say we have found something in each other?"

Ava's hand gently ran down his cheek to draw his lips closer to hers. "At first I was frightened by it. The longer we've been together, my fears crumbled. I've never been like this." She lightly pressed her lips to his. When their lips parted and they shared a breath, forehead to forehead, she sighed. "I've never been able to look a man in the eyes like this. Your eyes are golden to me, their heat absolutely

161

tantalizes me." She blushed and turned her face. "Am I sounding mushy now?"

Hank caught her chin and returned her gaze to his. "Mushy? Never. You're helping me understand everything I feel for you." He held her with her cheek on his chest. "Hear that old heart of mine?" Ava's finger drew circles in his chest hair. "It beats for you now."

Ava's sigh released a long breath. "Imagine two people like us, weathering cruel winters in our lives, only to get here, where we have so much ahead of us."

Hank's breathing hitched at her declaration. Now if only she could or would admit this out of bed, fully dressed. He knew he could.

****

Ava had to work fast. First she hoped her lawyer, Victor, would speak to her. Then she had to map out her plan. Why did she work so hard? To survive, to get on with life, to earn a living. Did she have to do that now? No. The interviews for an event manager were glowing with candidates. It would be a crush until Sky and Conner's wedding, but the future was worth it.

Chapter Fourteen

At sunset, Ava, Jordan, and Kameo boarded the runabout for the Mele Lani resort. As they drew closer, the massive pink castle seemed to rise out of the ocean.

Ava turned to Jordan. "Good night, nurse. How did I miss knowing about this place? Hank was right when he said it floated on the waves."

Jordan sat gobsmacked at the illusion of the castle in the darkening sunset. Kameo nodded in awe. "Someone went to a lot of trouble to keep such a beautiful resort off the map."

Ava cocked her head. "But why?"

Jordan nodded wisely. "Secrets."

All three women raised their brows. Kameo, used to wearing a white coat over scrubs, smiled at the apricot-and-peridot native print of her dress.

Jordan snickered. "We look like extras from *Blue Hawaii*."

Ava smoothed the traditional island dress across her lap. "Hank said the hotel staff wears this print. Something about the green matching Mrs. Hiatt's eyes."

Jordan smoothed back a lock of hair. "I spent the day on the phone, getting Chinese interpreters for those who wish to seek asylum in the United States."

The two women made a wincing face. Kameo drew a deep breath. "Oh, yeah, fourteen pages of a form to explain the twelve-page application the person completes."

The boat docked. Ava nodded toward the pink palace. "The pocket folders were delivered this morning. They hold info about money, food, shelter, medical care, and communication with their families back home."

Jordan nodded. "Along with how to get home if they desire. I found out that in China there's little sympathy for people who were trafficked. They're considered to be prostitutes, even if it was against their will. Many won't want to return."

Under the halo of the dock light, two people stood close together. Ava nodded ahead. "Is that Mr. and Mrs. Hiatt?"

Kameo shrugged. "Guess we'll find out."

Resort staff extended a hand to help them alight to the dock, and they were escorted to the young couple. "I'm Rick Hiatt," the young, fresh-faced man bore none of the typical island tan. He enthusiastically extended a hand. "This is my wife, Anna. We're tickled to meet you. This is going to be quite a night, isn't it?" Rick's expression gleamed with anticipation.

Anna stepped forward, her long, titian hair up in a high ponytail, but it still whipped around her snow-white neck. "When Rick told me what you were doing, I said, I want to help."

Ava glanced at Anna's vividly green eyes. She had never seen eyes so clear and bright. "Hank told me the green in this fabric matched your eyes. It certainly does."

Anna tucked her chin. "Oh, thank you. The color is a favorite of Rick's."

At being introduced to Jordan, Anna winked. "You're Conner's step-mom?"

Jordan looked from Ava to Kameo. "I am. How do you know Conner? Has he flown for you?"

Anna paused and her hand flew to her cheek. "Oh, Sky Kingston's art is all over this resort. My friend, Cat, is one of her biggest fans because of the life studies Sky's done."

Kameo tilted her head in curiosity. "Life studies?"

Rick nodded. "If seeing those nudes doesn't send a man right back to the gym, I don't know what would."

Kameo and Jordan gulped at each other. Jordon nodded. "Oh, those life studies, those were done a while ago."

Rick brought them back to the subject of the evening. "Have you dined?" He checked his watch. "I had the chef prepare food for sixty. I thought some of the companions might need a hearty meal. There's plenty if you'd like to enjoy his menu."

Ava smiled. "Oh, we've eaten, but if I'm here for any length of time, I might get peckish."

As Rick and Anna led them into the resort, he grinned. "I have not heard that expression in ages." Rick gestured for them to follow him down a long hall and into an area marked employees only. "This is the staff cafeteria. We've set up a station for you, Dr. Roman, and wrangled a nurse from our dispensary to assist you. We've stacked the folders you sent over at the intake table. Your interpreters have arrived." He nodded to three people enjoying dinner at a long table. "I think you'll find everything you need here, if not speak up."

Jordan's gaze swept the room. "Any chance we'll see the aquarium room?"

Rick's body language affirmed her request. "Kirk did mention I need to keep you from it, lest you demand one for yourself."

Jordan shook her head. "That's just not fair."

Anna raised a well-manicured brow. "I think I can make that happen. I haven't promised anyone anything."

Ava regarded the gracious surroundings of the employee cafeteria. "Perhaps some tea while we're waiting for all hell to break loose?"

Anna guided her toward a well-appointed beverage station. "We have a number of proprietary tea blends; would you like something stronger?"

Ava was struck by the abundance of teas and coffees. "I'm sure I'll find something here I like." *I have catered nice affairs. I have walked into multimillion-dollar mansions. I've never seen employees this well taken care of.*

As Ava made a small pot of tea, she watched Rick and Anna chat with Jordan and Kameo before Rick excused himself. Ava stood stirring the tea until she thought she'd grind out the bottom of the cup. *Those two can't be older than Conner and Sky. They must use excellent sunscreen, maybe they're really forty-five. I, on the other hand, am the sun-loving crypt keeper.* Ava shrugged as she sipped an exotic tea. *He has to have family money. With Evan Silver's recommendation, Hiatt is certainly good at what he does.*

Chapter Fifteen

Peng's body tingled at the thought of what might await. Tonight was a triumph. *They played right into my hands and now I will experience…* By the end of this evening, he would have his membership. He would become a *valued* member. He already saw some changes he thought he'd make. *Art is an excellent way to launder money. I could turn these pieces into a goldmine. There are far too many male nudes. I'll replace them with females and launder a King's ransom.*

Peng Huang strutted into the card room like he owned the place. It was a plush room. Carmine-red-silk wallpaper met black walnut-planked floors. Over-padded leather chairs ringed the long, oval table. One corner held a conversation area with tobacco-colored-leather sofas and marble-top tables. *This bar is impressive.* Peng surveyed the area and recognized many of the whiskey brands he also served.

One of the gorilla twins flanked him with Kirk at Peng's right hand. He gestured into chairs the two lovely Asian women walking a respectful distance behind them. When they each raised their heads and their eyes widened at the scope of this card room, he returned a chastising glare. Their heads bowed in supplication.

The General greeted Peng. "My estimation of you has just increased tenfold. You kept your word."

Peng narrowed his eyes and bowed from the shoulder. "Of course. I always keep my word." He nodded to Ronnie. "Good evening, Syaoran. He threaded his fingers and flexed. "I've come here to play cards and win."

Ronnie Tengfeng cocked his head. "Just to play cards? I thought you wanted to experience everything that is Mele Lani."

Peng backpedaled. "I am here as your guest. I thank you for whatever hospitality you extend."

Ronnie led him up to the bar where the General stood with two strangers. He introduced one young man as Rick Hiatt. The muscular fellow was Jax, the dealer.

Ronnie took control. "It will be a gentlemen's only game tonight, though I see you have brought feminine entertainment. When the time is right, we'll break for that."

Peng was impressed when they brought his favorite whiskey without his requesting it. "My stable was escorted to a waiting area by your staff. I understand companions are held for health screening. You'll find all my people very healthy, but I appreciate your thoroughness. Perhaps we could do some trading?"

Peng turned to scrutinize the opulent card room. The dominant lighting came from a Dale Chihuly chandelier over the game table. "General, that piece of glass over the table is quite a bold choice, with all the room's traditional elegance."

The General winked at Rick Hiatt before he responded. "That is the spirit of Mele Lani. Tradition *and* kink. Don't you think it looks like an octopus?"

Peng shrugged. The General swished the ice cubes in his glass and double doors at the back of the room opened. A parade of leather-clad kinksters sashayed along the room's perimeter. It was a long parade. Men and women carrying crops or being led by leashes gave the players brazen smiles. One woman in black knee-boots and a leather bikini came to stand in front of Hank, stroking the thongs of a deep red flogger. "Good evening, Bambi. You're looking well tonight." He caressed the leather thongs and turned to Peng. "So, what's your kink?"

Peng looked around the room at the selection of subjects. With a pompous sneer, he replied. "Blood play, but alas, none of the island clubs support that."

Rick spoke right up. "I do enjoy that here."

Ronnie's gaze bounced from Rick to the General and back to Peng. "Oh, we have that... But permission for blood play relies on your complete honesty in our next game."

Peng nodded to the waiting table. "Poker is not a game of honesty—"

Ronnie cut him off. "Ah, my friend. You agreed to a game of truth or dare. We play this first." Ronnie nodded to the dealer. "Give us the room, please."

The lean, muscled dealer nodded and left. Standing at the bar, Rick produced a sealed deck of cards. "Gentlemen, high card issues the command."

Ronnie opened the box, shuffled the deck, and offered it. "As the guest, you draw first."

Peng drew the top card and smirked as he turned it over. "King of diamonds."

Ronnie inclined his head and turned over the next card. "Ace of clubs."

Hank gestured to the sofas along one wall. "Let's play in comfort." Bambi followed Hank and sat at his feet. The others fell into place, and the room's tension was palpable.

Ronnie challenged. "Do you desire truth or dare?"

Peng sat rigidly. "Dare."

Ronnie posed thoughtfully; his eyes closed for a beat. "I dare you to let Ms. Bambi apply nipple clamps on you for the evening."

Peng stared incredulously. "I've changed my mind... I choose truth."

The men laughed at him, bringing a scowl to his face. Ronnie inclined his head. "I could insist that a choice is a choice. You should know we could hold you down while Bambi applies those nipple clamps." Ronnie's tongue swept over his upper lip. Glancing sideways, he drew his knuckle to his teeth. Making eye contact with the General, Ronnie sniffed and exhaled. "I'm in a generous mood tonight and every act at Mele Lani is consensual. Do you agree, Peng?"

Peng drew air through his teeth. "Is my answer my truth?"

Ronnie's brows knit as he drew himself to sit taller. "No. Your truth question is do each of your companions come to you of their own free will?"

Peng smirked. "How would they know the joys I have to offer if they don't know about me, and I never force their hands?"

The General chuckled. "I hear you there, my friend." Hank leaned back into his chair and sobered. "I know what I do to break in a new lovely." He abruptly sat forward and mirrored Peng's tented fingers. "Tell me how you school your impressive stable."

Peng eased onto the leather couch; his arm extended along the back as he expounded his sadistic wisdom. "I take a page from de Sade, the philosopher. I start with isolation. I move on to total control of all their bodily functions. Food, water, bathroom, sleep. It only takes a matter of days. My longest holdout was ten days. Unfortunately, she had to be put down."

Rick shifted in his chair and looked away, grinding his jaw. Peng sneered. "Perhaps you don't have the stomach for training?"

Rick's gaze narrowed as his lips drew a straight line. "You may be right. So, tell me, have you lost any other companions?"

Peng sniffed. "It's a small percentage, but that's business. I bring in two hundred companions a month. Some are lost, most are sold, some cannot handle the honor and take their own lives."

As the room chilled at his callousness, the General nodded toward Peng conspiratorially. "Two hundred men and women a month. How extraordinary! With that kind of operation, I believe you and I could do business together."

Peng, sensing he had the upper hand, pressed his luck. "If you made it worth my while… Say $100,000.00 per virgin?"

Hank blinked. "$100,00.00 per virgin. How many virgins are with you tonight?"

Peng smiled. "Five."

The General sat back for a beat. "Do the virgins get this money?"

Peng laughed uproariously. "Do you give money to your racehorses? Thoroughbreds have many expenses. The money covers my fees."

Hank exchanged a long look with Rick. "Mr. Hiatt, would you do the honors for this transaction?"

With a swift nod, Rick approached the cashier and returned with $500,000.00 in cash. The mound covered the coffee table nicely. "I would be pleased if you would count it."

Peng leaned forward and inspected each banded stack, and quickly counted fifty stacks out loud. "The exact amount agreed upon."

Hank extended a hand. "Handshake on our agreement?"

Peng extended his hand. "Five hundred thousand dollars in cash for five virgins."

Hank settled. "I was all prepared to show you my entire operation tonight and here we end up doing business. Now I have to ask, how do you manage this volume of people? Surely not entirely on your own?"

Rick questioned. "You must have rivals. How do you deal with them?"

"Mr. Hiatt, do you know who my family is? My father and his father before him were ambassadors from the People's Republic. My father ran our operation before he stepped up as an ambassador. One day, I'll take his position in the government. You must understand, we do so much more than the flesh trade."

Rick blinked and turned to the General. "Diversification is the key!"

Peng tapped the arm of the sofa. "Counterfeiting, drugs, guns… we have a pleasant life."

Ronnie's posture shifted as he sipped the last of his drink. He smiled genially. "How do you explain your income for taxes?"

Peng boasted. "We launder it primarily through art, jewels, and real estate. And there is always the Maldives."

"I don't know how you pull it off." Ronnie's grin spread. "The IIT will be very interested in this information."

Rick raised innocent eyes. "The IIT?"

Ronnie's gaze turned cold. "The equivalent of your IRS in China."

Peng started to rise, blustering. "You can't be serious."

Ronnie's smile turned frigid. "Oh, I am very serious. This room has video cameras and has recorded your confessions. Oh, my incorrigible friend, when you harassed your neighbor, the wedding planner, you set your downfall into play. This month, you are on The Vesper with your chattel and your father is in the halls of government. Next month, you will all be residents of a Xinjiang internment camp, possibly not as pleasant." Ronnie turned to the General and Rick. "They don't sound terribly comfortable. I imagine our guest will try to find his way out of here."

On cue, Peng snapped his fingers. The lone gorilla brother hulked toward the men. Kirk gave him a dismissive sneer. "You'll only get hurt. Plus, you're in America, you do not have diplomatic immunity, but you can save yourself by testifying against Peng." Kirk threw up both hands. "Peng, I'm out."

Peng and the gorilla brother watched Kirk leave the room unmolested. "What is this?" Peng exclaimed as realization hit the gorilla brother and he caught up to Kirk.

Rick looked at Hank as he held his forefinger and thumb an inch apart. "You must be this smart to recognize this is a sting."

Hank nodded to Rick, rose from his seat, and approached Peng. "What you did to Ava Hansen was unconscionable. But what you've admitted to now will bring dishonor to the Huang name and probably get you killed." Hank spread his stance and balanced on the balls of his feet, scrubbing his hands together. "Let this be your lesson, don't fuck with someone just because you think you can. See where it ends?" Peng rose in the small space Hank afforded him and initiated a martial art pose. "And now this? You're going to get yourself hurt." Hank stepped back, allowing Peng room to spring into an attack. Effortlessly, Hank stuck out his foot and Peng hit the carpet. Hank took a knee and pressed his thumb into Peng's neck at the carotid. "You see these men around me? They are all far more skilled at close-quarters combat than you. So, if you did manage to defeat me, which is unlikely. You'll never make it out of this room."

Ronnie and Rick stood over Peng as the man introduced as the dealer re-entered the room, carrying cuffs and shackles. With a confident stroll, the muscled man in the tux joined the others over him. "Is your little tantrum worth a broken neck?"

Ronnie gave the guy a high five. "Jax, so good of you to join us."

Jax handed Ronnie the cuffs and shackles and struck his usual hands-on-hips pose. He smirked. "Well, I thought you fellas had it under control." He nodded to Ronnie. "You do the honors."

As Peng was led out, Hank raised a brow at Jax. "What kept you?"

Jax shrugged and chuckled. "Number two gorilla brother thought he'd cause a ruckus in the cafeteria." He turned to Rick. "I was headed over to him with a can of whoop-ass, but man, your wife packs quite a punch. She put him down as if he were a fly."

Rick nodded. "She is… something."

"Who was her trainer?" Jax pressed. "I want to study with that guy."

Rick laughed outright. "Actually, that guy is a gal named Venus. Her daddy taught her how to defend herself and she just passes that along."

Chapter Sixteen

Dawn broke over the flamingo-colored resort as the participants of the evening trickled into the aquarium room by ones and twos. Rick and Anna quietly supervised the staff as they set up various food stations. The elevator doors opened, and Jordan gasped as Kirk led her into the room. "Did you set up breakfast in this special room just for me?"

Anna smiled. "That way, I figured you had to see it."

Rick stood comfortably in his bare feet. "Breakfast is the most important meal of the day. I'm ravenous when I rise."

Ava pinched Hank and whispered. "There's a guy after your own heart."

Rick caught her gaze with a boyishly wicked smile. Rick gestured to the fragrant food stations. "Make your choices and have a seat. Last night was a triumph. I'm anxious to learn the outcomes."

When everyone was gathered around the table with drinks and food in hand, Hank gazed curiously at their host and hostess. "Aren't you eating with us?"

Rick smiled. "We keep nocturnal hours; I hate to rest on a full stomach."

Anna placed her hand over his. "But we simply could not rest until we hear everything that happened."

Hank stirred his celery stalk in his Bloody Mary. "I received a call from Ronnie. The government of the People's Republic sent a jet to fly him and Peng back to justice. Ronnie carried the videos of not only their wayward son's confession but forty-eight video statements from their kidnapped citizens."

Rick pursed his lips. "It's disturbingly fascinating that the crime of tax evasion was what caught their eye."

Jax nodded to his server and smiled. "Oh, by the by, the Coast Guard is outside right now, towing off The Vesper and placing her crew under arrest."

Hank smirked. "Nice boat. Maybe one of us can win it at a property auction.

Kirk looked across the table and shook his head. "You know what a boat is. A hole in the water where you pour money."

Ava tisked. "Besides, there's not enough sage in the world to purify what they did there."

Hank looked up from his steak and eggs. "So, where are all the companions?"

Ava raised her mimosa. "Thanks to your wonderful skills at poker, we were able to buy out a boutique hotel until they get on their feet."

Kameo looked toward Ava. "Once I spoke with a few of them, I realized Peng had abducted many from universities. There are some brilliant people in this group." She scowled down at her plate. "I hope they do shoot Peng."

Jax raised his glass to Anna. "This one is another woman I don't want to cross. She can be bloodthirsty."

Anna smiled serenely. "I can understand that urge."

Kirk glanced at Jordan, who stared at sea life with fascination. "You here with us, babe?"

"I was just fantasizing about swimming along with the turtles."

Rick's smile brightened. "You are welcome to swim with them whenever you please."

"I'll remember that offer. Thank you so much." She refocused. "I sent the Health Department to that sorry excuse for a dormitory they were using. The police will go with them and arrest the guards."

Hank sat sipping his drink with great satisfaction. "How will we know when the entire Huang family is back in China?"

Jax winked. "Don't worry about that. Ronnie will give us a call. From what he said, it shouldn't be longer than a day or two."

Servers approached the table with trays of goblets holding an effervescent red wine. When everyone had a glass, a server brought Rick and Anna their glasses. "Before we head upstairs, I want to share a toast to your successes." The diners held their glasses, waiting for his toast. "This is a zesty sparkling shiraz." Ava regarded the interesting red bubbles as Rick began his toast. "Here's to long life and prosperity, to all of your posterity; and those that don't drink with sincerity, may they be damned to eternity."

Anna withheld a chuckle. "Nice touch, Fitz."

****

As the helicopter pulled away from Mele Lani, Ava let out a long sigh and glanced around at the group. "It's such a shame we can't have Sky and Conner's wedding here. Sky's art is all over the place…"

Hank squelched a belly laugh. "Did you get the nickel tour? Or the fifty-cent tour?" His knowing gaze swept the men as they kept straight-faced.

"I saw the cafeteria and the aquarium room, the bathrooms were posh, the entire place screams elegance." Ava shrugged.

Kameo slapped Jax's shoulder and leered at him, but Jax spoke up. "The place screams alright, but it has to do with all the leather and discipline."

Ava's eyes grew wide as her mouth oh'd. "Perhaps the Royal Hawaiian is best."

Jax caught Kameo's hand and kissed it. "Maybe Conner and Sky can spend a couple of nights on their honeymoon there…"

Hank lowered his Ray-Bans. "You're talking about my daughter…"

****

The rumbling of the elevator intruded on Ava's thought process. *This mess is over. Once the police realize who was on the other side of the wall, my insurance claim should go through without a hitch. I can find a new office and restock a warehouse. I'm back in business.* She closed her eyes tightly and drew in a breath as they arrived at Hank's condo.

Hank keyed the code on the front door. "Have I shared my code with you?"

Ava snapped into the present. "No, is that twenty-first-century language for giving me a key to your place?"

Hank opened the door and gestured her in. "I guess is it. I don't even have a key."

The portent of his words made her entire body blush. She walked into his arms and rested her head on his chest. "Oh, handsome, this has been such a hurricane. How can I ever thank everyone for going to bat for me?"

They stood in the front hall, rocking within their embrace. Hank smoothed back a lock of her hair. "Ah, them? They're the loophole gang."

She looked up at him. "The what gang?"

"The Roman family will jump through any loophole to right a wrong." He chuckled. "It's kind of fun. Isn't it?"

"Aside from losing all my professional assets, it was a real thrill ride."

Hank cupped her chin. "You were only worried because you didn't know us well enough then. Our family will never let you down."

She wrested from his embrace and ambled aimlessly around his condo living room. "The kids are happy here." She ran a hand up the stalk of the tallest bird of paradise plant. "That's good to know."

Hank cocked his head at her. "Sunshine, what's up?"

"I'm still processing everything. I've got to rebuild a business. Your daughter's wedding needs attention. I have other projects and you have an aviation company to start. When are we going to have time for each other?" Her head hung, her hands wringing.

Hank drew in a deep breath. "Like everyone else does, early mornings, late nights, stolen lunchtimes."

She hugged herself. "I've got to get home and sleep for about a day." She looked up at him guiltily. "I'm sorry, just need some me time." Stepping back, she waved him away.

Head hung low; Hank held out a hand. "Let me drive you across the canal."

****

Hank shook his head at her response at the condo complex's front door. She didn't want him to walk her up. She had her key in her hand from the moment she sat in his car. Hank *thought* they'd had a meeting of the hearts. Hank *thought* they were a couple. *I'm being silly. It's just a day of alone time.* He looked at himself in the rearview mirror. *I could use a day of sleep myself.*

****

The next morning, Hank woke to phone calls from his contractor. "Oh, you caught me off guard. I've had a string of late nights, Noa. Sorry about those missed calls."

Hank heard it in the man's voice. Noa's patience rode the edge of a knife. "General, you need to come out here and see our progress. We're ready for the next stage."

Hank abruptly sat up in bed. "I thought Conner was keeping an eye on things."

"He is." Noa agreed. "But it's your name on our contract and I need your sign-off."

Hank stared at the clock. "How about 1000 hours?"

There was a protracted silence. "Sure, if that's the best you can do."

After Hank closed the call, he took a shower for clarity's sake. *Back to normal. Time to refocus.* Shower, shave, and hit the day.

Before he slid his wallet into his pocket, he dialed Ava. There was noise in the background as she answered.

"Good morning, handsome. What are you doing?"

"Ahh, got to ride out to the hangar. I have to work today."

"Funny how that happens. I'm touring light industrial warehouses today."

He heard her step away from the noise. "This time, get friendlier neighbors."

"Right, I'm going to interview them as rigorously as the management office screens me." There was a beat of silence and they both spoke at the same time.

"I miss you."

They both answered. "You do?"

Ava covered the phone's mouthpiece, and he heard her muffled voice. She returned to their call. "I'm back. What's up?"

"Sunshine, how about dinner tonight? I'm buying."

"Ooh, okay. I'll text you when I get out of this meeting. Okay?"

"Good deal." Hank smiled as he drove across the island to Kingston Air.

****

Conner paced as Hank approached from the parking lot. "Were you abducted by aliens? Have you checked your messages at home?"

Hank scoffed. "I was working on your wedding, you ungrateful welp." He playfully caught Conner around the neck with his elbow and shook him. "What does Noa need me for? To sign his checks?"

Conner shrugged out of the hold and smoothed his polo shirt. "Big decision here, family bathrooms or one for each? Changing table or none?" The men walked toward the aviation office.

Hank squinted, imagining the options. "We're flying families for lots of money. So upscale, separate bathrooms with changing tables in both."

Conner halted mid-step. "You're one of them?"

Hank snorted. "One of them what? Fathers? Yeah, your time will come, kid."

Conner shook his head. "I won't clean number two."

Hank threw an arm around his future son's shoulders. "Keep that thought in your man-place because once you put a ring on Sky's finger, you'll be one of us. And when that precious baby looks at you, squirms, and cries, but Sky is worn out? You'll change that poopy diaper and grin at the kid while you do it."

****

Catching a sandwich at lunchtime was the loneliest thing Hank had done since he got to Hawaii. *This is reality. Wake up, work, eat, go to bed. Damn. I thought this was paradise.*

****

The rest of the summer went on with boring predictability. By August first the flights for Kingston Air ran without a hiccup. Hank and Conner, however, were about to hire more pilots to cover 'date nights'.

"Thursday for dinner?" Ava read from her calendar.

"What about breakfast?" Hank countered.

"Can you sleepover Wednesday night?" Ava begged.

"I've got a late flight to the Big Island." Hank sighed.

****

If Ava's August soundtrack was 'Hello, Goodbye', to Hank it felt more like 'The End'.

"Sunshine, it's been three days since we've seen each other. Want to set up semaphore flags on the lanai?" He heard Ava's chair creak along with her heavy sigh, then her steps, and a heavy door opening and slamming.

"I can't tell if you're being sarcastic or practical." She sounded on edge. "Hank, I'm tied up through Sunday evening. The larger warehouse and the extra help I've hired has just added more events."

Hank sat at his desk, fully aware of Kingston Air's arrivals and departures. "Ava, where does that leave us?" Hank heard a forklift in the background, Ava's hand covered the receiver as she barked a list of directions. She came back to their conversation. "Okay, we were talking about Sunday?"

"You were. I've got a sunrise flight to the Big Island Monday. I can talk to Conner if that's the only time you've got for me." *That sounds whiny.*

There was a clash of something formidable in the background and Ava yelped a stream of curse words he'd never heard from her. "Hank, let me call you back."

If Hank was doing the decision two-step, Ava was doing a dance of the hours.

Chapter Seventeen

The Thursday before Labor Day, Hank landed his Tecnam P2012 Traveller at 1100 hours. He drove directly to the Royal Hawaiian resort with the final numbers and payment for Sky's wedding and reception. By now, the hotel staff was used to his smiling face. Many of his charter clients were guests of the resort.

Hank sat at a corner table for two in the resort bar and grill, his knee bouncing with nerves. There was something about a pilot's uniform that drew nods and smiles as the other diners acknowledged him. He looked down at the shiny name badge, Captain Kingston, and smiled. Everything was coming together. *Well, almost everything.* There was one mission left to complete. He lifted his hat off the booth seat just to check that the small ring box was still under it. *Idiot, I just it put there, where would it go?*

Hank heard Ava's 'in charge' voice from a distance. He recognized the tone. He heard it every Sunday night after dinner when she returned to her condo. He enjoyed weekends, especially when she didn't have a Friday night event. That was date night. Today was business, and he had to be on her calendar to see her.

With a crinkle of shopping bags, Ava swept around the corner and grinned effusively at him. "Handsome, where have you been?"

Hank rose and greeted her with a massive hug. "The Big Island. Just got back. What's in those bags?"

She kissed him squarely on his lips and sweetened the deal when she split his lips with her tongue. He held her in place, enjoying the sparkle in her azure eyes, and resisted letting her go. She gave him a little shake, and they snapped out of the very public demonstration of affection. She glanced at the bags and got back to business. "Wedding goodies for the bridal party. They arrived this morning." They sat, and she pushed the bags toward Hank. "Can you deliver them to Sky?"

Hank nodded as the waiter came by. It was a perfunctory visit. Hank and Ava ate the same things every week. As their dishes were brought out, Ava sat back and let out a heavy sigh. "Less than thirty days and your Peanut will be Mrs. Conner Roman-Jamison."

Hank swallowed a bite and chuckled. "I just call him the Big Nut, I have ever since they called me to announce their engagement. It's not like this isn't just a formality, but it's a great way to celebrate them."

Ava rested an elbow on the table, her chin in her hand. "What a great start they have. When Conner told me how they met, I thought this is a fairy tale. How many people live a fairy tale?" She sealed that question with a wink.

"Aww, do you really want to dance till midnight and lose one of your expensive shoes?"

"Not one of my shoes." Ava paused. "It didn't bother you it took them four years to get married? Is marriage just a formality?"

Hank pursed his lips. "Not for me, but they had definite ideas, and they followed them. If it were me? I'm old enough to know my heart. How about you?"

Ava stopped mid-slurp, a noodle passing between her lips. "Wait, what?"

Hank's brow rose as he put down his iced tea. "Have you gotten any of the psychic messages I've been sending you? After the wedding, will I ever see you again? I had to make this appointment to see you today."

Ava blinked. "We see each other…" She stopped a beat and took a slow draw on her straw. "But… I miss you. It would be nice to be together more, you know, just together with nothing in particular to do…"

Hank nodded. "I'm glad to hear you say that. I'm thrilled to know I don't have to keep booking events…"

Now Ava softened. "Yeah, I was working on a surprise for you at Sky's wedding…"

"I get that." Hank nodded, oblivious. "Then let me book a big event with you." Ava stared before she resumed eating. "It's like this. I want a small wedding, a small reception, a short honeymoon…

Ava swallowed and shook her head. "But you just paid for Sky and Conner to …"

Hank smoothly produced a ring box and dropped to one knee. "And I want a wonderfully long life together, Ava."

Ava hid behind her napkin. "I, ah, I… you mean for us?"

Hank looked around the room as people stared. "I'm not on this floor for nothing, Sunshine."

Ava stood and hurried him up into a hug. "What took you so long?"

Hank placed the sparkler on her finger. "I had to get on your calendar."

They cuddled as much as a newly engaged couple could in a restaurant at noon. Ava whispered in his ear. "I know you really love me."

Hank agreed. "I really do. I have from the day I helped you off that ridiculous luggage carousel."

"As it happens, I've been working on something for us and I have a favor to call in with the license agent at this resort."

Hank blinked. "But who do we get to hitch us up?"

"They owe me a favor, too. If we talk fast, we can be married by nine AM."

Hank wagged his brows. "The shorter the wedding, the longer the honeymoon." Ava blushed.

****

Ava woke at the sound of something heavy falling in the next room. She wiped the sleep from her eyes and the first thing she saw was her wedding dress bag hanging on the closet door. *This is really happening.* She rolled over in the king-sized bed and Hank was missing. There was another thump and his distinctive line of cusswords. She rose and tied on her robe to discover the hubbub was from the third bedroom, which still functioned as Hank's file and storage room. *This really needs to be converted to his office… our offices.*

When she lightly knocked on the door, Hank answered softly. "Sunshine, I'm sorry I woke you up."

Opening the door a crack, their gazes met, and Ava could see he was a different Hank than she'd seen in their past. "Are you okay?" She hung at the doorframe, watching him sitting cross-legged in the center of the room. Pictures and papers were stacked around him. "Did you find the papers you need?"

Hank gave the paper a second look and nodded. "Yeah, the death certificate. It took me for a long walk down memory lane." He shook his head. "Have a seat, Sunshine." He gestured to a bench of stacked boxes. Once she sat, his smile emerged. "Seeing these," he held up his original marriage license and his wife's death certificate, "made me a little emotional. It brought back the dizziness of being young and getting married and having everything ahead of you." He waved the death certificate. "And this? This was like a death sentence for me, too. Man, I nearly ran off the rails. I fought with God, I fought with guys in bars. I drank. I thought of every reason in the world to not go home at night until my sister-in-law had Sky in bed."

Ava got off the boxes and sat with him on the floor. She ran the backs of her fingers over his cheek and notice his dried tears. "That had to be a catastrophic time for you."

"But I had a toddler who didn't understand anything. I guess at that point, I didn't understand death myself. I was lucky I had a commanding officer who reached in and pulled me out of the pit. He gave me about three weeks of idiocy and then he rode me hard and held me to all the standards I'd met before. I won't say it was easy, but he saved me. He saved my relationship with my daughter."

Ava felt a wave of emotion from him he'd never shared before. She put her arm around his back. "And look where you are now."

Hank dropped the papers and drew Ava into his lap. "I don't know where I'd be today if I had taken a military transport to Honolulu."

Ava blushed. "Aww, handsome, are you getting mushy?"

Hank fell to his back and Ava giggled as she rolled on top of him. "Mushy? Nope, just thinking about my fairy tale."

Ava straddled his waist and playfully patted his chest. "We can't start the honeymoon until we're married."

Hank looked around the room. "Right, we have to get to the resort's license agent to do that. But first, at our age, how do we get off the floor?"

Ava shook her head at him. "Where is my poker-playing James Bond?"

"That kid, Hiatt, schooled me on my character's persona in about fifteen minutes. James Bond wasn't reality, welcome to the real, real."

Ava smirked back and playfully slapped his shoulder. "I heard all about 'the General' with his girl on a leash. I think you enjoyed that way too much." She struggled to her feet and held out a hand. "Come on Pa, it's time to tie the knot."

Hank gracefully rolled to his knees and rose. "Okay, Ma, I'm a-coming."

****

As Hank slapped on a little cologne before leaving the bedroom, he heard Ava in the living room changing her voice mail greeting. "This is Ava. I can't come to the phone right now. I have a plot twist. I'm getting married today! If you absolutely have to reach me, I'll be at the Royal Hawaiian. I'll be checking messages around noon."

****

The woman's name badge said Sadie Lancaster; by her accent, she came to Honolulu by way of Wales. As Ava and Hank entered her office, she dithered along, speaking to herself until Hank cleared his throat.

She gave him a deer in the headlights stare after she looked him over from head to toe. "Ava, dear, is this your young man?"

Ava bit her lip. *Of all the days for the supervisor to be out of the office, I chose this day to get married.* "Why yes, he is. Hank, this is Sadie."

Sadie grinned girlishly as she nodded to Ava. "Well, aren't you dressed to the nines to see me today?"

Hank looked at the boutonniere and Ava's corsage in the plastic clamshell. "We thought it would be a great day to get married."

Sadie got out from behind her desk and walked around Ava. She touched Ava on the forearm and stood back to admire the dress. As she circled the couple, she nodded and talked to herself. "Simply stunning. Ah, what a luxurious lace… and look at your skirt, how those pleats are… so alluring." Sadie got close to Ava's hair and squinted. "Is that Swarovski in your comb?" Ava nodded.

Hank felt like he was on cadet inspection. He bobbed his head at Sadie. "What, am I in rags over here?" His thumbs rode under his lapels to emphasize the trim cut of his suit.

Sadie stuck her head around Ava and waggled her fingers at him. "Such a handsome catch you have. No wonder you're a vision in pale gold. Ha! Of course you are. You wouldn't be dressed like this for business."

If only Sadie had clarity of mind, that would please Ava greatly. Sadie didn't. Sadie was lost in the lace and satin of Ava's bridal finery.

Hank stepped forward. "How do you do?" Sadie nodded as he presented the paperwork to her. "We completed the application and we've got the papers you need."

Sadie flipped through the stack. "What is this? A death certificate? A declaration of death? I've never handled one of these… Oh." Her excited sigh melted to disappointment.

Ava, having watched dozens of these transactions, stepped to Sadie's side. "It's very simple, dear. It's just like a death certificate…"

"But is it… legally?" Sadie slid off her readers, hanging on the chain around her neck. They bounced on her generous bosom.

Ava and Hank nodded, prodding the idea into Sadie's consciousness. Ava pointed a manicured nail. "But it is a legal document allowing me to marry him." She pointed to Hank as he shifted impatiently.

Sadie confessed. "I need to call my supervisor. He doesn't come in until ten today."

Ava dug for her cell phone. "I can get him now." Sadie's expression brightened. Ava's call rang to voicemail. Everyone hovered tensely. Ava dialed again. This time, a strange voice answered, and Ava rolled over his hello. "Kai, I'm sorry to call you, but we have a wedding emergency." Kai's answer was barely intelligible as Ava put it on speaker. "Have you had an accident?" There was the sound of a drill and water running."

A strange voice spoke. "This is Dr. Jones; Kai has a mouthful of Novocain; he can't speak to anyone right now."

Ava sighed. "I'm sorry. When will he be done?"

The dentist took a beat and reasoned. "About nine-thirty. I'll have him call you."

Ava closed the call. "Sadie, isn't there anyone else you can call? Perhaps the agent at the next resort?"

Sadie sat, chastised. "Oh, no, it has to come from Kai."

Hank turned to Ava. "Sunshine, let's do what Kai can't do, have a little breakfast and come back at ten."

****

At ten o'clock, Hank swept open the door to the license office. Five pairs of accusing eyes shifted to him. Kirk, Conner, and Jax paced a circle in the small office as Jordan and Sky sat shoulder to shoulder, involved in a low conversation. When Hank and Ava filled the doorframe, Sky leapt at her dad. "What are you doing here without us?"

Kirk stopped mid-step and barked. "What's the rush? Is she pregnant?"

Jordan covered her face with her hands. "Kirk Roman, that's rude."

Ava waved Kirk away. "I can see the headlines now, mid-fifties woman pregnant in Honolulu."

Hank looked at each of them. "We didn't want to make a big fuss. We did this spur of the moment."

Jordan shook her head. "Spur of the moment? You woke up and decided to get married?"

Hank and Ava grinned at each other. "No, it was the topic of conversation at lunch yesterday. If it hadn't been for confusing paperwork, you would have missed us this morning. You guys are holding up the wings of progress."

Hank nodded as Ava headed toward a thirty-something man with a swollen jaw. "Kai, when I called, I had no idea where you were.

I'm sorry. Does it hurt much?" He nodded, his eyes sad. "Can you issue the license?"

Sadie spoke up. "Once Kai came in and looked at your papers, he had me complete this." She held the license closely. "Sixty-five dollars, please."

Hank felt for his wallet and opened it. "Here you go, exact change." He looked back at his friends. "Who wants to watch a wedding?"

****

Kai's final words came out through numb lips. "Ih now pronoun you maa an wi. You may kith the bri…"

As Hank swept Ava into a grand embrace, Kirk elbowed Jordan. "Is any of this ceremony legal?"

Jordan wiped away what could have been tears of laughter. "It was so beautiful, in that weird train-wreck kind of way."

Kirk applauded while the other four just gawked at him. When he stopped clapping, he recovered with an offer. "Lunch is on me."

****

Kirk walked with his hand at Jordan's back as they entered the very exclusive restaurant known as Chef Hilo's. "Teflon, did you honestly book this yesterday?"

"Believe it or not." Hank grinned evilly. "When I was picking up the tab for a small bridal lunch, I'll admit it was for two. But you spoke up, and they accepted the change of party as we drove over. Thanks for our reception, Romeo." Once the hostess led them to the large round table, Hank chided. "Hey, Romeo, we missed the mandatory twenty percent gratuity by one person."

Kirk shook his head as he sat and spread the napkin across his lap. No sooner than everyone was settled, a server wheeled a tall masterpiece of a seafood tower toward them and lifted it to the center of the table. "How much is this setting me back?"

191

Hank got out his phone and went to the calculator. "I'll keep track, Romeo." They proceeded with everyone enjoying the selection of food on the tower.

Jax urged Hank to eat another raw oyster. "That's the last one, catch it while you can." He wagged his eyebrows at the groom.

Ava spoke up as she passed another plate to Jordan. "Too much food and I'll fall asleep before the big show."

"Ah, yes, the big show." Jordan nearly choked on her drink.

The men narrowed their gazes at the two women. Kirk inclined his head to Hank. "Hey, buddy, I'll pony up for twelve more oysters."

Hank wiped his mouth with his napkin. "I'm good, seriously. You heard the lady. We can feed each other leftovers in the morning."

When the server rolled out the small wedding cake, everyone applauded. Standing together, both holding the knife, they cut the first piece of the Haupia Pineapple Crepe Cake. Hank held the bite on a fork. "Okay, Mrs. Kingston, open wide."

With loving pride, they fed each other the multilayer crepe cake without wearing it. Ava leaned against him and whispered to Hank, "This cake is almost as tasty as you."

Hank's cheeks flushed. He caught her around the waist and turned their backs to the crowd. "Aww, cut it out, Sunshine." He pulled her into him and raised a brow. "Do you think they need to see the launch sequence begin?" Ava giggled and looked over his shoulder at the table.

Sensing the vibe, Kirk announced. "We better send these two love birds home before they scare the children." He wagged his brows at Conner. "We've come to the honeymoon portion of today's show and it's time for us to go."

****

At the Royal Hawaiian Resort, the staff beat a path to wait on the new couple with gushing enthusiasm. When the elevator opened on the top floor, the bellman mentioned. "There are only two suites on this floor. They are each our finest bridal suites. Both feature the Waikiki view and sunsets are positively magical here."

He opened the room full of exotic plants and flowers. On the table in the living room sat a basket of fruit, champagne in a chiller, and he could see robes across their king-sized bed in the next room.

Hank slipped a gratuity into the bellman's hand, and they were alone. Magically alone.

Hank hooked the do not disturb sign on the door and threw every lock. "May I interest you in a champagne cocktail, Mrs. Kingston?"

Ava lowered her chin and arched her brow as she stepped out of her crystal-covered pumps. "Alcohol, now? Let that chill. We have a deal to seal." She nodded toward the bedroom with the Diamondhead view.

"Now I know why I'll call you my better half." Hank loosened his tie as he followed her into the bedroom. "The way I see it, if I follow you, I'll always have a great view."

She shook her head as she turned and slid off his suit coat. "Okay, sweet talker. Let's see how you do with zippers." She turned and lifted her hair from the back of the dress.

"I am a zipper aficionado." Hank bent first to kiss her neck. As she melted against him, he whispered in her ear. "I'm also the luckiest bastard on earth."

They stayed in that position, smoldering before their next steps. "Handsome, I'm the luckiest woman." He unzipped her dress with kisses at every inch as it revealed her tanned skin. She shivered as the dress dropped to the floor. Ava turned, arms out. "How do you like my lingerie?"

Hank stood admiring her as he unbuttoned his shirt sleeves. "I don't know what you call each piece, but together, it's like whipped cream on a wedding cake."

"You like the thigh-high stockings?" She placed a stockinged foot on the end of the bed and struck a pose.

Hank swallowed hard. "Now there you go, making it impossible for me to concentrate on getting undressed.

She walked seductively back to him. "That was never my intent." Her fingers flew over fabric Hank was too distracted to handle. His breath hitched as she not so cautiously ripped his belt from the loops and groaning with anticipation as her hand slipped to hold his trousers. She unbuttoned them and slid down the zipper slowly. "Did you get enough to eat at the reception, or are you hungry for more?"

Trousers hit the floor with a jingle of change and keys, and Hank sat on the end of the bed to slide out of his shoes and socks. "If I asked you to keep those stockings on, would you think that was a little too kinky?"

Ava pushed him back onto the bed. "Let me free the girls, and I promise to keep the stockings." With one hand behind her back, she unclipped her bra, and it slid down her arms. Hank caught it and brought it to his nose. "I get to have you for the rest of my life, good Lord." He crooked his finger at her. "I'll take off your panties if you remove my shorts."

She was on him like hot fudge on a sundae, warm, soothing, and surrounding him. She bit her bottom lip as she revealed all of him. "Umm mmm yummy."

Hank's hands fell to her hips and the lacy high-cut panties. "These are just too pretty to rip; I want to see these on you at least once a week."

Ava sucked in a breath as her panties joined his shorts on the floor. "Now that we're naked, what can we do?" She started to walk to her side of the bed. Hank playfully grabbed her and fell back in the middle of the mattress. While he held her to him, he blessed her with kisses across her collarbone and up her neck. They stopped, their foreheads together, mesmerized by each other. "You know, we need to take this nice and slow because I want to remember this forever."

Hank grinned as they moved up to the pillows. "My daddy used to say, 'what I did all night, now takes all night to do.' So, chances of slow are on our side."

Ava squelched a laugh. "How can you talk like that?"

Hank shrugged as he moved to her side and propped himself on his elbow. "Truth in advertising."

"Will being with you always be this much fun?"

Hank considered. "There will be nights when we play strip poker." He gestured at them. "But tonight, I'm all in." He moved to roll over her.

"You're not all in yet." Ava slid her legs wider, and he was as good as home.

"What, you want to pass up foreplay?" His fingers trailed through her center and her back arched toward him.

"Oh, hell, no… not the way you do it…"

****

"Then lose the shoes," he commanded quietly.

He didn't have to ask twice. Her wedding dress had served its purpose. Now it cuddled on the floor with his trousers. Ava sucked in a shaky breath, waiting for what came next, the anticipation so keen she could barely contain herself. She trembled.

Ava smiled at the flush flowering across her breasts. She felt the heat spiking along her skin in tingles. She reveled in what he did to her. She needed him; he needed her, and their need was overwhelming. Judging by Hank's ardor, she knew they would not be denied.

He pulled her tight against him, branding her body with his. "This will be like nothing we've ever experienced before," he warned with a sly smile.

Her brow arched. "Oh? Why?"

"This is married sex. And we can spend all day in bed because we have the license. It's all about worshipping each other. I made that vow." Before she could respond, his lips descended on hers.

Longing, so often denied, burst like chrysanthemum fireworks, tendrils of light separating and splaying brightly behind her closed eyes. They devoured each other with their lips and their tongues. Masterful hands searched and found, felt, and explored. An unexpected sigh of peace escaped Ava's lips as if she'd finally come home in his arms. *Did he feel it, too?*

****

The usual clear-crystal blue of her eyes was smoky tonight, as focused like lasers. "I need to feel you, too," she insisted and skated her palm over his chest. They couldn't stop touching each other, their brakes were off. Her palm rubbed firmly against his anxious erection, and within a breath, he quivered within her touch.

Hank's urgency flowed through him, blinding him to everything else. She melted for him. Lord, she was so hot, her skin contained the molten heat of vitality, and he wanted her more desperately than anything he'd ever known.

Ava surrendered to him in an all-consuming kiss. Every other thought flew from his mind. The crisp coolness of the fresh sheets invited him to play. Hank broke the kiss and hovered over her on his elbows. Her azure eyes burned for him. "I want you, Hank," she declared urgently, arching against him. "I want you. Tell me you want me."

"I do," he groaned, "Ava, from the first minute…" His mouth was on hers again. His lips sought her sweet flesh along the delicate silk of her cheek and the long column of her neck. She moaned and arched again, wrapping arms and legs around him, holding him close. He broke her hold easily to continue his passionate exploration of each breast, each nipple.

She whimpered his name hungrily. "Hank…" Just his name, but the loving way she said it spoke volumes.

Lord, she tasted like…what was that? The flavor eluded him. *Cherries? Yes, cherries.* He remembered their sweet, sharp taste from childhood. She smelled of them, tasted of them. He recalled being young, careless, and free. His heart soared. And more, oh my, her musk, that essence her body made just for him. Hank inhaled leisurely and cocked a smile at Ava beneath him. "I'm gonna fuck you every way there is. I'm gonna make you come so hard, you'll see stars. That's how your husband fucks."

****

She couldn't speak. She knew he meant it. She held his gaze until his eyes left hers and focused on the dusky triangle between her legs. Then she shut her eyes and just let him have his way. Her legs began to tremble as he spread the petals of her sex with those long, strong fingers.

He studied her for a moment. "Such a pretty pussy," he murmured admiringly. "I'm gonna eat this pussy every chance I get for the rest of our lives." His tongue swept along her flesh and her moans of pleasure echoed his. His tongue slid up to her clit and focused there, followed by his lips.

****

Hank admitted to himself that he had an unfair advantage. His lack of sheet time had nothing to do with his skills with women. It had everything to do with having no women to romance. So, in the desert, he laid back on that RV bed and imagined what he would do with a goddess of his own.

Her hips bowed up to him urgently, seeking his lips, and he was desperate to please her. He smiled and obliged, feeling her shudders and the rhythmic roll of her hips. Ava's fingers spasmed in his hair, pulling tightly as he brought her release, then caressing him gently as the waves of intensity drifted away. Her legs dropped open, and her hands rested limply against him as she cuddled into his embrace.

Hank reveled in it all, every sensation, every taste, every response. He took his time studying her, learning what brought her the greatest pleasure. He whispered, "I need to be inside you."

Ava smiled serenely. "Then come to me."

Oh, God, it was incredible. Like coming home. This surge of love, longing, and tenderness flavored with passion, desire, and abandon. They fit perfectly. Her body embraced him like the ultimate hug. He felt the fine, light sweat of her effort and her pleasure blossom across her body. More, he sensed their love enveloping him. Love he knew was there since their first kiss.

****

Their world together had changed. Ava felt it. She felt Hank knew it, too. She admitted to herself what she'd known from the moment he sat down on that barstool. She loved that this man was so tender and strong at the same time. His focused tension inside her naturally drew her closer to him. Her body met his instinctual call and answered.

Ecstasy consumed them. This frenzy grew stronger as he lay beside her. When had she ever felt such love? *Never with anyone.* He was spent, there within her arms. She smoothed his damp brow and his eyes flickered open with a boyish smile. She whispered. "Hank, I cherish the day you walked into my life."

He rallied to throw both arms around her and sighed, his toes still curled. "What did I tell you about meeting you earlier?" She nodded. "I only regret we didn't meet sooner, so I could love you longer." They fell into a rapturous deep sleep that even the brilliant Waikiki sunset didn't budge.

****

The next morning, when the champagne bubbles were gone and the bridal energy was spent, Hank rolled to his feet and blinked, feeling every muscle. *Did I come back from maneuvers last night?* He stretched and let out a lion's yawn. Looking at his left hand, he grinned. *Yup, I got her.* He strolled naked around the suite and played with some newfangled coffee pot. Without directions, he searched for where tab A went into slot B. Knees bent; he got closer to read the fine print and abruptly two hands caught his hips and he startled, jumping straight up. "What the ever-living hell?"

Ava wiped her sleepy eyes. "I have a coffee pot just like that. Go back to bed and I'll bring my husband some coffee."

Hank moseyed into the bathroom, and before he closed the door, he quipped. "Don't let your boyfriend know."

When he nearly limped out of the bathroom in his robe, he picked up a hotel pamphlet. "Wifey, how about we call these eager young massage therapists and order one of these couples' massages?"

Ava leaned against the coffee station and grinned eagerly. "Coffee first. Then a shower to wash the sex off."

Hank scratched his head and gave it a thought. "Do you suppose they think we were in here playing monopoly all night?"

Ava started preparing the mugs. "It will take weeks for them to get our musk out of here, but we don't need to advertise it."

Hank nodded and dialed the number for the spa.

****

After being massaged into heaven and back, Hank and Ava reclined with spring water on the lanai. He watched her through half closed eyes. Where he was limp with relaxation, she was bottled excitement. "What's up, Sunshine?"

"I did a thing…" She giggled in response.

He caught her hand and kissed her ring finger. "Yes, we did."

"Weeks before that, I called Victor and had him draw up papers on my business." Hank's lips pursed as he nodded. "Once the kids are married, I'm stepping back. I've got a gal I worked with in Vegas flying out next Wednesday. Iolani Kamaka will shadow me and then the Monday after the wedding Iolani's lovely head will wear the heavy crown. I'll be just the name at the top of the letterhead."

Hank's eyes widened. "But you love your job."

"I'm in the next stage of life. Thanks to a huge check from Sheldon's life insurance, I don't have to work another day. You married a wealthy woman."

Hank sat up, his legs crossed before him. "Is that a fact?" He shook his head and took a deep breath. "Lucky me."

Ava got up, walked around the chaise, and sat in his lap. "And you proposed before you knew that!" Ava booped his nose and then kissed him soundly. Their honeymoon continued.

Chapter Eighteen

It was a warm September morning in paradise. Sky and Conner's wedding programs sat waiting at the back of the resort's patio. Ava's staff hurried along, bustling to get every floral arrangement in place for the outdoor wedding. The arch of orchids stood waiting for the moment when Hank would hand Sky over to Conner Roman-Jamison.

In the bridal suite upstairs, Ava grinned as she watched everything down below. This was the same suite she and Hank enjoyed on their brief honeymoon. She sat at the foot of the bed and blushed. The three bridesmaids giggled as they poured another glass of Blanc de Bleu Brut for Sky's Aunt Sherry. Sherry patted the sofa. "Ava, your people have this. Relax, you need to sit and have a drink with me."

Ava fidgeted as the hairdressers and makeup artists moved with the efficacy of a SEAL team. "I know. I have to breathe. Honestly, I'm not like this when it's other people's events." She looked at her watch. "It's nine-thirty. The photographer will be here shortly to take photos." She gestured to the exquisite Hawaiian wedding dress hanging and ready for its portrait. Stopping to enjoy the bridesmaids' fragrant pastel plumeria bouquets, Ava arranged them on the foyer's round table. She tinkered with the ribbons of Sky's bouquet that matched her Haku Lei. "Once they take photos, these flowers can go back in the cooler," she said to no one in particular. Staring at the center of the table, Ava cried out. "Where *is* Sky's Haku Lei?"

Sherry got up from the sofa and followed Ava's plaintive cry. "I don't know what that is."

Ava dithered. "It's her headpiece!" Her hands fisted in anxiety. "Where the hell is her headpiece?" She pinched her walkie-talkie. "Iolani, where is the Haku lei? You know white dendrobium orchids, plumeria, and orange blossoms. I don't see it up here." *I'm having a 'mother of the bride' meltdown. Now I understand these women.*

The walkie-talkie squawked back. "It's with the men. The General is going to bring it to the bride right before he walks her down."

Ava collapsed in a chair, her mood lightening. "Oh, I forgot about that." Sherry walked up with Ava's glass and a fresh bottle of the delightful pale-blue sparkling wine. "Have some of this. It's the strongest thing we've got."

Ava accepted the glass and cocked her head. "Why aren't you nervous? You raised her."

Sherry dismissed that comment. "Yeah, but for the last five years, I sat back and watched Hank take over. And everything looks under control to me."

****

Hank stood beside Conner as they straightened the pleated lines of their Havana shirts before they slid into their linen suit jackets. "These are a lot better than the monkey suits you guys looked at."

Conner snickered as they fidgeted in the mirror. "Yeah, a barefoot wedding is the way to go." He searched the room for his groomsman and dad. He turned back to Hank. "Where's my best man? Has he planted whoopie cushions on the white chairs just for fun?"

Kirk passed by and patted Conner's shoulder. "Don't worry, Jax can act normal when the occasion calls for it. I don't believe the cartel was on the invitation list."

Conner shook his head. "From the sound of it, maybe the gorilla brothers should have guarded the gift table."

He turned to his father and sighed. "In a couple of hours, I'll be a married man. I never thought that would happen."

Kirk smirked and slapped his back. "No one ever does, son."

Hank leveled him a look. "But you are *committed* to my daughter, right?"

Conner sobered and then grinned. "If the past few years haven't proven that, I don't know what would." His expression turned quizzical. "Do I get marriage credit for all the time we've been together?"

Hank and Kirk shook their heads and answered simultaneously. "No."

****

By eleven-thirty, the bridesmaids and groomsmen had their photos taken, and the suite was returned to its pre-hurricane state. Ava touched up her lipstick as Sky paced back and forth before the long row of balcony glass doors.

"Shouldn't I be nervous?" Sky asked her virtually new step-mom.

"Honey, you, and Conner are an evenly yoked pair. You guys finish each other's sentences. What's to be nervous about? You're marrying your best friend." Ava smoothed Sky's updo. "If I were you, I'd be excited about that first-class flight to Rome. Then you have your painting course in Florence and that marvelous thirteen-day cruise from Rome to Fort Lauderdale."

Sky's expression brightened. "And with your help, I'm packed for all of it. Daddy laughs every time he hears me mention that Louis Vuitton trunk. I don't know what it is about that trunk he finds so funny."

Ava took the anxious bride's hands in hers. "Your Daddy has one strange sense of humor."

****

203

They were interrupted by a knock on the door. When Ava opened it, Hank stood in his crisp, white-linen suit holding Sky's flowered headpiece. "Somebody here need a long walk?"

Sky squealed, "Daddy…" She picked up the front of her dress and ran to the foyer. "Have you seen Conner? He isn't hungover, is he? Did Jax get him drunk?"

Hank put down the flowers and caught both her hands. "Romeo reeled in Jax's leash. Between him and Kameo, damages were kept to a minimum. Conner's down the hall practicing his vows."

Ava waggled her fingers. "I'll be downstairs." She left bobby pins on the ledge below the foyer mirror and closed the door quietly behind her.

The room was silent, save for the sounds of waves crashing and children playing on the beach below. "Aww, Peanut." Hank walked Sky over to the balcony doors. They gazed at the never-ending waves. "It was just yesterday, we were like them." He pointed to a father and young daughter escaping waves on the shore. "It's really true that time evaporates. I just want these last minutes with you."

"Oh, Daddy, thank you for everything. You've been the best daddy a girl could want."

"It's been a real adventure with you, kid. Especially these last few years. You are quite a gal. I think Conner recognizes that."

Sky playfully stomped a bare foot and giggled. "He better."

"Oh, he does." Hank looked at the wreath. "Is it up to me to crown you with this?" Hank looked around the large, empty suite. "Where's all the help?"

"Daddy, I've never seen anything you couldn't do." She led him back to the mirror.

Sky stood centered and ready as Hank stood behind her with the Haku lei. Once it was situated, Sky pinned the wreath securely. Hank capped her shoulders with his hands and their gazes met in the mirror.

"I almost forgot; Aunt Sherry brought this from your mother's jewelry box." Hank dug in his pocket and pulled out a gold ankle bracelet with an aquamarine stone dangling from the center. "I got this for your Mom on her first birthday after we were married."

Sky's hand flew to her mouth. "I remember this. Aunt Sherry caught me playing with a box of Mom's things when I was about five. She told me they were putting it up until I was older."

Hank shrugged. "I guess we all forgot about it. Anyway, this is your something old and blue."

Sky sat down and put her foot on the hassock. "It's perfect with the side slit of my skirt."

Hank dropped to one knee to close the clasp around her ankle. Once he saw it glittering against her tan skin, he stopped and blinked. He ran his handkerchief under his nose and smiled up at Sky. "You're every bit as beautiful as she was, Peanut." There was a beat of silence between them. Hank rose slowly and extended a hand for Sky. "No amount of preparation can ever leave a man feeling ready to give his daughter away. But if I had to choose a person to hand you to, I would choose Conner every time.

****

Sunbeams broke through fluffy clouds, shining spotlights on their garden setting. The trio played traditional island music on their ukulele, bamboo drums, and a Xaphoon. The reeded instrument gave the music a low, rich sound.

The crowd hushed when Conner, Jax, and the two groomsmen came from the wings to stand beside the officiant. The wedding procession began with Kirk walking Aunt Sherry and her husband to the front row. After the bridesmaids collected at the bridal arch, the crowd circulated giggles at the sight of the pit bull mix with a ring box tied to his plumeria collar. The dog stopped mid-aisle and gave the crowd a suspect look. The best man, Jax, pulled treats out of his pocket. He hissed, "Doobie, over here. Now." The dog took a moment to scratch and then trotted between Conner and his master.

There was a pause, then guitars strummed the Hawaiian Wedding song and guests rose for the bride. Murmurs of admiration rippled through the crowd as Hank and Sky strolled toward Conner. Women sighed at Sky's gown, a twist on traditional island dresses. With her artistic vision, she chose to wear the creamiest pastel-peach sateen instead of white. Her golden-tanned skin glowed against the off-the-shoulder fitted bodice and demi-sleeves. The skirt was a bouquet of re-embroidered, deep-green monstera and maile leaves, embellished with white-orchid appliqués nestled among the leaves. A glimpse of tan leg peeked through the side slit to show off her gold ankle bracelet and coral pedicure. She was a graceful garden of color and fragrance as Conner stepped down to meet her.

With one hand on Sky's shoulder and one hand on Conner's, Hank leaned into Conner's space. "You're on your own, you big nut."

****

Their vows ended with them both saying, "As long as we both shall live." The officiant turned them to the crowd and announced. "For the first time anywhere… I present Mr. and Mrs. Conner Roman-Jamison."

Epilogue

The auctioneer barked, "The auction of each storage unit is open. There are no sealed bids. The unit is sold to the highest bidder. The winning bid must be paid in cash upon winning. The winning buyer is given twenty-four hours to clean out the unit or rent it under their name."

Hank mopped sweat from his neck as he waited impatiently for the auction staff to open the rolling door. *The last three units look like exploded toddler bedrooms.* He grumbled to Ava, "You honestly find decorative items for your events at these things?"

Ava gushed. "I have found some of the most glamorous things in storage units. Hawaii is like that. People move or they stop paying for them."

Hank shook his head and answered petulantly. "I could have been snorkeling."

"I promise we'll get to the beach after this one. Thank you for coming with me, handsome. 'Cause if we find things, I'll need muscle to help me move it."

Hank looked down at her. "You're trying to appeal to my masculine ego. Sadly, it's working."

Ava beamed up at him. "You're such a good husband."

"Keep saying that, Sunshine." As the lock fell to the ground, the door went up.

Hank whistled as he looked over the shoulders of the shorter bidders. He heard plenty of groans at the unmarked skids full of boxes still wrapped in dusty poly wrap. Sitting forlornly on the top of the furthermost skid was a pair of chandeliers. *Are they crystal? Are they trash?* Everything was coated with months of dust.

Ava squinted. "I like those chandeliers; we could use a pair. The way everything is in boxes could mean the items were wrapped with care." She rose on her toes and whispered. "I want this one."

One group of parents seeking kids' things shuffled off. The more experienced resellers shook their heads at the unmarked boxes. It was down to Ava and two surly beach bums who had not won an auction yet.

"You sure, Sunshine?" Bids started at $250. The other two parties bickered at each other as the price rose to $500. Ava shifted against Hank uneasily. He nodded to her and bid. "$1000.00."

The beach bums scowled at him, waved him off, and declared. "You got it, old man."

The auctioneer pushed for more and Hank rolled his eyes. "One thousand, cash, today."

When the transaction was finished, Hank cut the poly wrap from the first skid. "We're going to need your truck. You'd better call Mano to come over."

Ava impatiently pulled at a box. "It's heavier than I thought." Hank plucked it from her and placed it on the ground. With a knife's slice, he opened the top. He looked up at the sky and howled. "I hope to God these didn't fall off a truck."

Ava bent over. "These are laptops. A bunch of laptops."

"Sunshine, these are iPad Pros. Maybe eighteen hundred dollars apiece."

As fast as Hank could put the boxes in front of Ava, she sliced them open to find some other high-end electronics. By the time Mano arrived with the panel truck, Hank handed Ava the dusty chandeliers. "Last two skids. One looks small."

She studied the chandeliers. "These look familiar, they could be European antiques."

Hank pulled a carton to the floor, and as Ava sliced it open, Mano pointed and yelped. "I know this box, see the tape, I resealed this. These are those devil shoes."

Ava fell back against the tall skid. "Those damn sneakers?"

Mano nodded actively as he pulled out a box. "One hundred and seventy-eight thousand dollars' worth of sneakers."

Hank looked at the shoes in Mano's hands. "Those are the shoes that started all your problems? They have got to be the ugliest things on Earth."

Ava belly laughed. "If my memory serves me right, you didn't think much of that Louis Vuitton trunk, either. I'm glad you fly planes for a living and don't run an appraisal business."

"There's no accounting for some people's tastes." Hank wiped the sweat off his forehead and gestured with his chin. "What's in those last three boxes?"

Each person picked up a box and peeled back the tape. Ava squealed. "My cake projectors!"

Ava and Hank watched as Mano drove away with their loot. The two beach bums ambled up. "What did you find, uncle? Fax machines?"

Hank poo-poohed his mother-load. "It was toner cartridges." Ava elicited a sad expression until the guys rode off on their bikes. She snuggled against Hank, her arms around his neck. "I think you've earned not only snorkeling, but kinky snorkeling."

Hank drew up to his full height. "I'll call Rick and tell them to send the helicopter from Mele Lani."

THE END

DO YOU ENJOY TEA?

Find our custom blended teas at Adagio Teas
www.adagio.com, Signature Blends

Hau'oli / She Lives Aloha

Low caffeine, purchase benefits Hawaii Foodbank

Blended With Apple Pieces, Rooibos Tea, Pu-Erh Tea, Rose Hips, Hibiscus, Orange, Lemon Verbena, Dragonfruit Flavor, Strawberries, Pineapple Pieces, Dragonfruit, Natural Orange Flavor, Cocoa Nibs, Natural Strawberry Flavor, Rose Petals, Marigold Flowers, Natural Creme Flavor & Natural Hazelnut Flavor. Accented With Cornflowers & Hibiscus Flower.

Winning Hand

Trace caffeine, purchase benefits International Justice Mission

Blended With Decaf Ceylon Tea, Pineapple Pieces, Coconut, Natural Pineapple Flavor, Natural Coconut Flavor, Decaf Ceylon, Apple Pieces, Natural Mango Flavor, Mango Pieces & Marigold Flowers. Accented With Coconut, Hibiscus Flower & Pineapple.

OTHER BOOKS BY AMBER ANTHONY

Paranormal Romance
Appetite for Blood*
Blood Rising*
Blood Emerald*
Blood Dragon*
Blood Fugue
Blood Legacy

Metaphysical Fiction/Romance
Arise, My Darling

Contemporary Romance
Becoming Gabriel

Action/Adventure Romance
Roman's Revenge
Roman's Rules
Roman's Return

Seasoned Romance
Roman's Rules
Roman Wedding

New Adult
Roman's Return

*Audiobook Available at Audible, Amazon, and iTunes

Praise for Amber Anthony

Roman's Revenge

"Amber Anthony generously doles out steamy romance, heart-pounding action, and edge-of-your-seat suspense."
-Amazon Customer

Roman's Rules

"Great characters and setting, with plenty of humor, fill another fun read for these terrific authors."
-Amazon Customer

Roman's Return

"So many connections that turn out with humor and quirky romance. The kind of family you wish you had, even when his brother, Jax is a dick of a big brother.
-Amazon Customer

Arise, My Darling

"Being an intuitive myself, I was hooked from the beginning."
-Amazon Customer

Becoming Gabriel

"The romantic buildup between Grace and Gabrielle was priceless. Multi-dimensional facets of the protagonists' personalities made the plot come alive for me.

The book has an old-world charm. There's a special kind of magic that happens when two people fall in love within impoverished settings. Their dire circumstances created a delightful tension which magnified their romantic encounters."
-Amazon Customer

Appetite for Blood

"A paranormal romance that has it all, and then some! When a prequel has you itching to read the trilogy, that's superb storytelling! … I'm a fan! Kudos, Amber Anthony!"

-Amazon Customer

Blood Rising

"Great world-building and complex characters add to an interesting story. Matt and Cat's attraction is deep and powerful. Their chemistry is very hot, and the love between them sweet, touching, and spicy. A plot that offers plenty of drama, suspense, danger, and passion."

-Amazon Customer

Blood Emerald

"Rick Hiatt is a hero to die for in this stunning standalone. Literally. We were first introduced to this devilishly handsome vampire in the first book of the Blood series. Now, Rick is the leading man in this second installment, and readers are going to melt as his story unfolds."

-Romantic Times, Top Pick 4.5 Stars

Blood Dragon

"Amber Anthony writes paranormal characters you'd like to have as friends. Bound by fierce loyalty, Adam and his colleagues, vampires Rick Hiatt and Matt Brenner (previous books), engage in the kind of good-natured ribbing and witty repartee that had me laughing out loud. Their devotion to their mates and the sizzling love scenes had me wistfully sighing."

-Amazon Customer

Blood Fugue

"Amber Anthony is a true master of paranormal romance. Another fantastic tale of love and turmoil. Her hero is reluctant and chivalrous. Her heroine is strong-minded and compassionate. Together, they find their way through the tribulations of the mind. To find true lasting love."

-Amazon Customer

Blood Legacy

I have read all of Amber Anthony's books. I mean every single one. So I wasn't going to pass up Blood Legacy (Tales from the Goaler Book 2). It was like getting together with old friends while making new ones.

The budding romance between vampire Gerry McIntosh and mortal woman Isla Cathcart presents some challenges (understatement), but it's when supernatural villains set up shop in Scotland that they really have something to worry about. Luckily, they don't have to face the threat alone. Vampire business partners Rick Hyatt and Matt Brenner re-unite with new business partner dragon shifter Adam Lachlan along with their very capable mates (Blood Series), to join forces with Gerry and Isla against a common enemy.

If supernatural abilities, a wealth of resources, indomitable style, and fierce loyalty to each other and new friends and allies weren't enough, the smart dialogue (teasing included) as written by Amber Anthony, is a joy to read whether you're a fan of paranormal stories or not. And I got a kick out of the tie-in to Amber Anthony's contemporary romance series, Roman's Adventures, with the mention of artist Skyler Kingston.

To know these characters is to love them. All I can say is, Amber Anthony, please keep bringing them back in new stories.

-Amazon Customer